The Hermit's Story

The Deer Pasture

Wild to the Heart

The Watch

Oil Notes

Winter

The Ninemile Wolves

Platte River

In the Loyal Mountains

The Lost Grizzlies

The Book of Yaak

The Sky, the Stars, the Wilderness

Where the Sea Used to Be

Fiber

The New Wolves

Brown Dog of the Yaak

Colter

The Hermit's Story

The Hermit's Story

STORIES BY RICK BASS

Houghton Mifflin Company BOSTON NEW YORK 2002

JUL 1 7 2002

Copyright © 2002 by Rick Bass

For information about permission to reproduce selections from
this book, write to Permissions, Houghton Mifflin Company,
215 Park Avenue South, New York, New York 10003.

Visit our Web site at www.houghtonmifflinbooks.com.

Library of Congress Cataloging-in-Publication Data

Bass, Rick, date.
    The hermit's story : stories / by Rick Bass.
        p.   cm.
    Contents: The hermit's story — Swans — The prisoners —
The fireman — The cave — Presidents' Day — Real town — Eating —
The distance — Two deer.
    ISBN 0-618-13932-X
    1. United States — Social life and customs — 20th century — Fiction. I. Title.
PS3552.A8213 H47   2002
813'.54 — dc21   2001051616

Book design by Anne Chalmers
Typefaces: Sabon, Cheltenham Light, Type Embellishments

Printed in the United States of America

QUM 10 9 8 7 6 5 4 3 2 1

Elizabeth

Acknowledgments

I'm very grateful to my family — Elizabeth, Mary Katherine, and Lowry — for their support, and to my editors who worked on these stories — Harry Foster, Camille Hykes, Elizabeth Kluckhohn, Tara Masih, and Alison Kerr Miller — and to Julie Burns for her help, as well, and to my agent, Bob Dattila, and typist, Angi Young. I'm proud to have Russell Chatham's painting on the cover, and I appreciate his cover design and the book design by Anne Chalmers. Thanks also for editorial help to George Plimpton, James Linville, Michael Griffith, and Lois Rosenthal, and to the editors of magazines in which these stories first appeared, in various forms: "The Hermit's Story," "The Cave," and "Two Deer" in the *Paris Review*; "Swans" in *Story*; "The Prisoners" in *Hayden's Ferry Review*; "The Fireman" in the *Kenyon Review*; "Presidents' Day" in *Southwest Review*; "Real Town" in *Epoch*; "Eating" in the *Southern Review*; and "The Distance" in the *Black Warrior Review*. "The Hermit's Story" and "The Fireman" also appeared in *The Best American Short Stories 1999* and *2001*, respectively, and "The Fireman" appeared in *Pushcart Prize 2002*.

These stories are based on the imagination and the characters in them do not represent any persons known to me, living or not.

Contents

The Hermit's Story

The Hermit's Story

AN ICE STORM, following seven days of snow; the vast fields and drifts of snow turning to sheets of glazed ice that shine and shimmer blue in the moonlight, as if the color is being fabricated not by the bending and absorption of light but by some chemical reaction within the glossy ice; as if the source of all blueness lies somewhere up here in the north — the core of it beneath one of those frozen fields; as if blue is a thing that emerges, in some parts of the world, from the soil itself, after the sun goes down.

Blue creeping up fissures and cracks from depths of several hundred feet; blue working its way up through the gleaming ribs of Ann's buried dogs; blue trailing like smoke from the dogs' empty eye sockets and nostrils — blue rising as if from deep-dug chimneys until it reaches the surface and spreads laterally and becomes entombed, or trapped — but still alive, and drifting — within those moonstruck fields of ice.

Blue like a scent trapped in the ice, waiting for some soft release, some thawing, so that it can continue spreading.

It's Thanksgiving. Susan and I are over at Ann and Roger's house for dinner. The storm has knocked out all the power down in town — it's a clear, cold, starry night, and if you were to climb one of the mountains on snowshoes and look forty miles south toward where town lies, instead of seeing the usual small scatterings of light — like fallen stars, stars sunken to the bottom of a lake, but still glowing — you would see nothing but darkness — a bowl of silence and darkness in balance for once with the mountains up here, rather than opposing or complementing our darkness, our peace.

As it is, we do not climb up on snowshoes to look down at the dark town — the power lines dragged down by the clutches of ice — but can tell instead just by the way there is no faint glow over the mountains to the south that the power is out: that this Thanksgiving, life for those in town is the same as it always is for us in the mountains, and it is a good feeling, a familial one, coming on the holiday as it does — though doubtless too the townspeople are feeling less snug and cozy about it than we are.

We've got our lanterns and candles burning. A fire's going in the stove, as it will all winter long and into the spring. Ann's dogs are asleep in their straw nests, breathing in that same blue light that is being exhaled from the skeletons of their ancestors just beneath and all around them. There is the faint smell of cold-storage meat — slabs and slabs of it — coming from down in the basement, and we have just finished off an entire chocolate pie and three bottles of wine. Roger, who does not know how to read, is examining the empty bottles, trying to read some of the words on the labels. He recognizes the words *the* and *in* and *USA*. It may be that he will never learn to read — that he will be unable to — but we are in no rush; he has all of his life to accomplish this. I for one believe that he will learn.

Ann has a story for us. It's about a fellow named Gray Owl, up in Canada, who owned half a dozen speckled German shorthaired pointers and who hired Ann to train them all at once. It was twenty years ago, she says — her last good job.

She worked the dogs all summer and into the autumn, and finally had them ready for field trials. She took them back up to Gray Owl — way up in Saskatchewan — driving all day and night in her old truck, which was old even then, with dogs piled up on top of one another, sleeping and snoring: dogs on her lap, dogs on the seat, dogs on the floorboard.

Ann was taking the dogs up there to show Gray Owl how to work them: how to take advantage of their newfound talents. She could be a sculptor or some other kind of artist, in that she speaks of her work as if the dogs are rough blocks of stone whose internal form exists already and is waiting only to be chiseled free and then released by her, beautiful, into the world.

Basically, in six months the dogs had been transformed from gangling, bouncing puppies into six wonderful hunters, and she needed to show their owner which characteristics to nurture, which ones to discourage. With all dogs, Ann said, there was a tendency, upon their leaving her tutelage, for a kind of chitinous encrustation to set in, a sort of oxidation, upon the dogs leaving her hands and being returned to someone less knowledgeable and passionate, less committed than she. It was as if there were a tendency for the dogs' greatness to disappear back into the stone.

So she went up there to give both the dogs and Gray Owl a checkout session. She drove with the heater on and the windows down; the cold Canadian air was invigorating, cleaner. She could smell the scent of the fir and spruce, and the damp alder and cottonwood leaves beneath the many feet of snow. We laughed at her when she said it, but she told us that up in Canada she could taste the fish in the water as she drove alongside creeks and rivers.

She got to Gray Owl's around midnight. He had a little

guest cabin but had not heated it for her, uncertain as to the day of her arrival, so she and the six dogs slept together on a cold mattress beneath mounds of elk hides: their last night together. She had brought a box of quail with which to work the dogs, and she built a small fire in the stove and set the box of quail next to it.

The quail muttered and cheeped all night and the stove popped and hissed and Ann and the dogs slept for twelve hours straight, as if submerged in another time, or as if everyone else in the world were submerged in time — and as if she and the dogs were pioneers, or survivors of some kind: upright and exploring the present, alive in the world, free of that strange chitin.

She spent a week up there, showing Gray Owl how his dogs worked. She said he scarcely recognized them afield, and that it took a few days just for him to get over his amazement. They worked the dogs both individually and, as Gray Owl came to understand and appreciate what Ann had crafted, in groups. They traveled across snowy hills on snowshoes, the sky the color of snow, so that often it was like moving through a dream, and, except for the rasp of the snowshoes beneath them and the pull of gravity, they might have believed they had ascended into some sky-place where all the world was snow.

They worked into the wind — north — whenever they could. Ann would carry birds in a pouch over her shoulder and from time to time would fling a startled bird out into that dreary, icy snowscape. The quail would fly off with great haste, a dark feathered buzz bomb disappearing quickly into the teeth of cold, and then Gray Owl and Ann and the dog, or dogs, would go find it, following it by scent only, as always.

Snot icicles would be hanging from the dogs' nostrils. They would always find the bird. The dog, or dogs, would point it, Gray Owl or Ann would step forward and flush it, and the beleaguered bird would leap into the sky again, and once more they would push on after it, pursuing that bird toward the horizon as if driving it with a whip. Whenever the bird wheeled and flew downwind, they'd quarter away from it, then get a mile or so downwind from it and push it back north.

When the quail finally became too exhausted to fly, Ann would pick it up from beneath the dogs' noses as they held point staunchly, put the tired bird in her game bag, and replace it with a fresh one, and off they'd go again. They carried their lunch in Gray Owl's daypack, as well as emergency supplies — a tent and some dry clothes — in case they should become lost, and around noon each day (they could rarely see the sun, only an eternal ice-white haze, so that they relied instead only on their internal rhythms) they would stop and make a pot of tea on the sputtering little gas stove. Sometimes one or two of the quail would die from exposure, and they would cook that on the stove and eat it out there in the tundra, tossing the feathers up into the wind as if to launch one more flight, and feeding the head, guts, and feet to the dogs.

Seen from above, their tracks might have seemed aimless and wandering rather than with the purpose, the focus that was burning hot in both their and the dogs' hearts. Perhaps someone viewing the tracks could have discerned the pattern, or perhaps not, but it did not matter, for their tracks — the patterns, direction, and tracing of them — were obscured by the drifting snow, sometimes within minutes after they were laid down.

Toward the end of the week, Ann said, they were finally running all six dogs at once, like a herd of silent wild horses through all that snow, and as she would be going home the next day there was no need to conserve any of the birds she had brought, and she was turning them loose several at a time: birds flying in all directions; the dogs, as ever, tracking them to the ends of the earth.

It was almost a whiteout that last day, and it was hard to keep track of all the dogs. Ann was sweating from the exertion as well as the tension of trying to keep an eye on, and evaluate, each dog, and the sweat was freezing on her as if she were developing an ice skin. She jokingly told Gray Owl that next time she was going to try to find a client who lived in Arizona, or even South America. Gray Owl smiled and then told her that they were lost, but no matter, the storm would clear in a day or two.

They knew it was getting near dusk — there was a faint dulling to the sheer whiteness, a kind of increasing heaviness in the air, a new density to the faint light around them — and the dogs slipped in and out of sight, working just at the edges of their vision.

The temperature was dropping as the north wind increased — "No question about which way south is," Gray Owl said, "so we'll turn around and walk south for three hours, and if we don't find a road, we'll make camp" — and now the dogs were coming back with frozen quail held gingerly in their mouths, for once the birds were dead, the dogs were allowed to retrieve them, though the dogs must have been puzzled that there had been no shots. Ann said she fired a few rounds of the cap pistol into the air to make the dogs think she had hit those birds. Surely they believed she was a goddess.

They turned and headed south — Ann with a bag of frozen birds over her shoulder, and the dogs, knowing that the hunt was over now, once again like a team of horses in harness, though wild and prancy.

After an hour of increasing discomfort — Ann's and Gray Owl's hands and feet numb, and ice beginning to form on the dogs' paws, so that the dogs were having to high-step — they came in day's last light to the edge of a wide clearing: a terrain that was remarkable and soothing for its lack of hills. It was a frozen lake, which meant — said Gray Owl — they had drifted west (or perhaps east) by as much as ten miles.

Ann said that Gray Owl looked tired and old and guilty, as would any host who had caused his guest some unasked-for inconvenience. They knelt down and began massaging the dogs' paws and then lit the little stove and held each dog's foot, one at a time, over the tiny blue flame to help it thaw out.

Gray Owl walked out to the edge of the lake ice and kicked at it with his foot, hoping to find fresh water beneath for the dogs; if they ate too much snow, especially after working so hard, they'd get violent diarrhea and might then become too weak to continue home the next day, or the next, or whenever the storm quit.

Ann said that she had barely been able to see Gray Owl's outline through the swirling snow, even though he was less than twenty yards away. He kicked once at the sheet of ice, the vast plate of it, with his heel, then disappeared below the ice.

Ann wanted to believe that she had blinked and lost sight of him, or that a gust of snow had swept past and hidden him, but it had been too fast, too total: she knew that the lake had swallowed him. She was sorry for Gray Owl, she said, and worried for his dogs — afraid they would try to follow his scent down into the icy lake and be lost as well — but what she had been most upset about, she said — to be perfectly honest — was that Gray Owl had been wearing the little daypack with the tent and emergency rations. She had it in her mind to try to save Gray Owl, and to try to keep the dogs from going through the ice, but if he drowned, she was going to have to figure out how to try to get that daypack off of the drowned man and set up the wet tent in the blizzard on the snowy prairie and then crawl inside and survive. She would have to go into the water naked, so that when she came back out — if she came back out — she would have dry clothes to put on.

The dogs came galloping up, seeming as large as deer or elk in that dim landscape against which there was nothing else to give the viewer a perspective, and Ann whoaed them right at the lake's edge, where they stopped immediately, as if they had suddenly been cast with a sheet of ice.

Ann knew the dogs would stay there forever, or until she released them, and it troubled her to think that if she drowned, they too would die — that they would stand there motionless, as she had commanded them, for as long as they could, until at some point — days later, perhaps — they would lie down, trembling with exhaustion — they might lick at some snow, for moisture — but that then the snows would cover them, and still they would remain there, chins resting on their front paws, staring straight ahead and unseeing into the storm, wondering where the scent of her had gone.

Ann eased out onto the ice. She followed the tracks until she came to the jagged hole in the ice through which Gray Owl had plunged. She was almost half again lighter than he, but she could feel the ice crackling beneath her own feet. It sounded different, too, in a way she could not place — it did not have the squeaky, percussive resonance of the lake-ice back home — and she wondered if Canadian ice froze differently or just sounded different.

She got down on all fours and crept closer to the hole. It was right at dusk. She peered down into the hole and dimly saw Gray Owl standing down there, waving his arms at her. He did not appear to be swimming. Slowly, she took one glove off and eased her bare hand down into the hole. She could find no water, and, tentatively, she reached deeper.

Gray Owl's hand found hers and he pulled her down in. Ice broke as she fell, but he caught her in his arms. She could smell the wood smoke in his jacket from the alder he burned in his cabin. There was no water at all, and it was warm beneath the ice.

"This happens a lot more than people realize," he said. "It's not really a phenomenon; it's just what happens. A cold snap comes in October, freezes a skin of ice over the lake — it's got to be a shallow one, almost a marsh. Then a snowfall comes, insulating the ice. The lake drains in fall and winter — percolates down through the soil" — he stamped the spongy ground beneath them — "but the ice up top remains. And nobody ever knows any different. People look out at the surface and think, *Aha, a frozen lake*." Gray Owl laughed.

"Did you know it would be like this?" Ann asked.

"No," he said. "I was looking for water. I just got lucky."

Ann walked back to shore beneath the ice to fetch her stove and to release the dogs from their whoa command. The dry lake was only about eight feet deep, but it grew shallow quickly closer to shore, so that Ann had to crouch to keep from bumping her head on the overhead ice, and then crawl; and then there was only space to wriggle, and to emerge she had to break the ice above her by bumping and then battering it with her head and elbows, struggling like some embryonic hatchling; and when she stood up, waist-deep amid sparkling shards of ice — it was nighttime now — the dogs barked ferociously at her, but they remained where she had ordered them. She was surprised at how far off course she was when she climbed out; she had traveled only twenty feet, but already the dogs were twice that far away from her. She knew humans had a poorly evolved, almost nonexistent sense of direction, but this error — over such a short distance — shocked her. It was as if there were in us a thing — an impulse, a catalyst — that denies our ever going straight to another thing. Like dogs working left and right into the wind, she thought, before converging on the scent.

Except that the dogs would not get lost, while she could easily imagine herself and Gray Owl getting lost beneath the lake, walking in circles forever, unable to find even the simplest of things: the shore.

She gathered the stove and dogs. She was tempted to try to go back in the way she had come out — it seemed so easy — but she considered the consequences of getting lost in the other direction, and instead followed her original tracks out to where Gray Owl had first dropped through the ice. It was true night now, and the blizzard was still blowing hard, plastering snow and ice around her face like a mask. The dogs did not want to go down into the hole, so she lowered them to Gray Owl and then climbed gratefully back down into the warmth herself.

The air was a thing of its own — recognizable as air, and breathable as such, but with a taste and odor, an essence, unlike any other air they'd ever breathed. It had a different density to it, so that smaller, shallower breaths were required; there was very much the feeling that if they breathed in too much of the strange, dense air, they would drown.

They wanted to explore the lake, and were thirsty, but it felt like a victory simply to be warm — or rather, not cold — and they were so exhausted that instead they made pallets out of the dead marsh grass that rustled around their ankles, and they slept curled up on the tiniest of hammocks, to keep from getting damp in the pockets and puddles of water that still lingered here and there.

All eight of them slept as if in a nest, heads and arms draped across other ribs and hips; and it was, said Ann, the best and deepest sleep she'd ever had — the sleep of hounds, the sleep of childhood. How long they slept, she never knew, for she wasn't sure, later, how much of their subsequent time they spent wandering beneath the lake, and then up on the prairie, homeward again, but when they awoke, it was still night, or night once more, and clearing, with bright stars visible through the porthole, their point of embarkation; and even from beneath the ice, in certain places where, for whatever reasons — temperature, oxygen content, wind scour — the ice was clear rather than glazed, they could see the spangling of stars, though more dimly; and strangely, rather than seeming to distance them from the stars, this phenomenon seemed to pull them closer, as if they were up in the stars, traveling the Milky Way, or as if the stars were embedded in the ice.

It was very cold outside — up above — and there was a steady stream, a current like a river, of the night's colder, heavier air plunging down though their porthole — as if trying to fill the empty lake with that frozen air — but there was also the hot muck of the earth's massive respirations breathing out warmth and being trapped and protected beneath that ice, so that there were warm currents doing battle with the lone cold current.

The result was that it was breezy down there, and the dogs' noses twitched in their sleep as the images brought by these scents painted themselves across their sleeping brains in the language we call dreams but which, for the dogs, was reality:

the scent of an owl *real,* not a dream; the scent of bear, cattail, willow, loon, *real,* even though they were sleeping, and even though those things were not visible, only over the next horizon.

The ice was contracting, groaning and cracking and squeaking up tighter, shrinking beneath the great cold — a concussive, grinding sound, as if giants were walking across the ice above — and it was this sound that awakened them. They snuggled in warmer among the rattly dried yellowing grasses and listened to the tremendous clashings, as if they were safe beneath the sea and were watching waves of starlight sweeping across their hiding place; or as if they were in some place, some position, where they could watch mountains being born.

After a while the moon came up and washed out the stars. The light was blue and silver and seemed, Ann said, to be like a living thing. It filled the sheet of ice just above their heads with a shimmering cobalt light, which again rippled as if the ice were moving, rather than the earth itself, with the moon tracking it — and like deer drawn by gravity getting up in the night to feed for an hour or so before settling back in, Gray Owl and Ann and the dogs rose from their nests of straw and began to travel.

"You didn't — you know — *engage?*" Susan asks, a little mischievously.

Ann shakes her head. "It was too cold," she says.

"But you would have, if it hadn't been so cold, right?" Susan asks, and Ann shrugs.

"He was an old man — in his fifties — he seemed old to me then, and the dogs were around. But yeah, there was something about it that made me think of . . . those things," she says, careful and precise as ever.

They walked a long way, Ann continues, eager to change

the subject. The air was damp down there, and whenever they'd get chilled, they'd stop and make a little fire out of a bundle of dry cattails. There were little pockets and puddles of swamp gas pooled in place, and sometimes a spark from the cattails would ignite one of those, and those little pockets of gas would light up like when you toss gas on a fire — explosions of brilliance, like flashbulbs, marsh pockets igniting like falling dominoes, or like children playing hopscotch — until a large enough flash-pocket was reached — sometimes thirty or forty yards away — that the puff of flame would blow a chimney-hole through the ice, venting the other pockets, and the fires would crackle out, the scent of grass smoke sweet in their lungs, and they could feel gusts of warmth from the little flickering fires, and currents of the colder, heavier air sliding down through the new vent-holes and pooling around their ankles. The moonlight would strafe down through those rents in the ice, and shards of moon-ice would be glittering and spinning like diamond-motes in those newly vented columns of moonlight; and they pushed on, still lost, but so alive.

The small explosions were fun, but they frightened the dogs, so Ann and Gray Owl lit twisted bundles of cattails and used them for torches to light their way, rather than building warming fires, though occasionally they would still pass though a pocket of methane and a stray ember would fall from their torches, and the whole chain of fire and light would begin again, culminating once more with a vent-hole being blown open and shards of glittering ice tumbling down into their lair . . .

What would it have looked like, seen from above — the orange blurrings of their wandering trail beneath the ice; and what would the sheet of lake-ice itself have looked like that night — throbbing with ice-bound, subterranean blue and orange light of moon and fire? But again, there was no one to view the spectacle: only the travelers themselves, and they had no perspective, no vantage from which to view or judge themselves. They were simply pushing on from one fire to the next, carrying their tiny torches.

They knew they were getting near a shore — the southern shore, they hoped, as they followed the glazed moon's lure above — when the dogs began to encounter shore birds that had somehow found their way beneath the ice through small fissures and rifts and were taking refuge in the cattails. Small winter birds — juncos, nuthatches, chickadees — skittered away from the smoky approach of their torches; only a few late-migrating (or winter-trapped) snipe held tight and steadfast; and the dogs began to race ahead of Gray Owl and Ann, working these familiar scents — blue and silver ghost-shadows of dog muscle weaving ahead through slants of moonlight.

The dogs emitted the odor of adrenaline when they worked, Ann said — a scent like damp, fresh-cut green hay — and with nowhere to vent, the odor was dense and thick around them, so that Ann wondered if it too might be flammable, like the methane — if in the dogs' passions they might literally immolate themselves.

They followed the dogs closely with their torches. The ceiling was low — about eight feet — so that the tips of their torches' flames seared the ice above them, leaving a drip behind them and transforming the milky, almost opaque cobalt and orange ice behind them, wherever they passed, into wandering ribbons of clear ice, translucent to the sky — a script of flame, or buried flame, ice-bound flame — and they hurried to keep up with the dogs.

Now the dogs had the snipe surrounded, as Ann told it,

and one by one the dogs went on point, each dog freezing as it pointed to the birds' hiding places, and Gray Owl moved in to flush the birds, which launched themselves with vigor against the roof of the ice above, fluttering like bats; but the snipe were too small, not powerful enough to break through those frozen four inches of water (though they could fly four thousand miles to South America each year and then back to Canada six months later — is freedom a lateral component, or a vertical one?), and as Gray Owl kicked at the clumps of frost-bent cat-tails where the snipe were hiding and they burst into flight, only to hit their heads on the ice above them, they came tumbling back down, raining limp and unconscious back to their soft grassy nests.

The dogs began retrieving them, carrying them gingerly, delicately — not caring for the taste of snipe, which ate only earthworms — and Ann and Gray Owl gathered the tiny birds from the dogs, placed them in their pockets, and continued on to the shore, chasing that moon, the ceiling lowering to six feet, then four, then to a crawlspace, and after they had bashed their way out and stepped back out into the frigid air, they tucked the still-unconscious snipe into little crooks in branches, up against the trunks of trees and off the ground, out of harm's way, and passed on, south — as if late in their own migration — while the snipe rested, warm and terrified and heart-fluttering, but saved, for now, against the trunks of those trees.

Long after Ann and Gray Owl and the pack of dogs had passed through, the birds would awaken, their bright, dark eyes luminous in the moonlight, and the first sight they would see would be the frozen marsh before them, with its chain of still-steaming vent-holes stretching back across all the way to the other shore. Perhaps these were birds that had been unable to migrate owing to injuries, or some genetic absence. Perhaps they had tried to migrate in the past but had found either their winter habitat destroyed or the path so fragmented and fraught with danger that it made more sense — to these few birds — to ignore the tuggings of the stars and seasons and instead to try to carve out new lives, new ways of being, even in such a stark and severe landscape: or rather, in a stark and severe period — knowing that lushness and bounty were still retained with that landscape, that it was only a phase, that better days would come. That in fact (the snipe knowing these things with their blood, ten million years in the world) the austere times were the very thing, the very imbalance, that would summon the resurrection of that frozen richness within the soil — if indeed that richness, that magic, that hope, did still exist beneath the ice and snow. Spring would come like its own green fire, if only the injured ones could hold on.

And what would the snipe think or remember, upon reawakening and finding themselves still in that desolate position, desolate place and time, but still alive, and with hope?

Would it seem to them that a thing like grace had passed through, as they slept — that a slender winding river of it had passed through and rewarded them for their faith and endurance?

Believing, stubbornly, that that green land beneath them would blossom once more. Maybe not soon; but again.

If the snipe survived, they would be among the first to see it. Perhaps they believed that the pack of dogs, and Gray Owl's and Ann's advancing torches, had only been one of winter's dreams. Even with the proof — the scribings — of grace's passage before them — the vent-holes still steaming — perhaps they believed it was a dream.

Gray Owl, Ann, and the dogs headed south for half a day until they reached the snow-scoured road on which they'd parked. The road looked different, Ann said, buried beneath snowdrifts, and they didn't know whether to turn east or west. The dogs chose west, and Gray Owl and Ann followed them. Two hours later they were back at their truck, and that night they were back at Gray Owl's cabin; by the next night Ann was home again.

She says that even now she still sometimes has dreams about being beneath the ice — about living beneath the ice — and that it seems to her as if she was down there for much longer than a day and a night; that instead she might have been gone for years.

It was twenty years ago, when it happened. Gray Owl has since died, and all those dogs are dead now, too. She is the only one who still carries — in the flesh, at any rate — the memory of that passage.

Ann would never discuss such a thing, but I suspect that it, that one day and night, helped give her a model for what things were like for her dogs when they were hunting and when they went on point: how the world must have appeared to them when they were in that trance, that blue zone, where the odors of things wrote their images across the dogs' hot brainpans. A zone where sight, and the appearance of things — *surfaces* — disappeared, and where instead their essence — the heat molecules of scent — was revealed, illuminated, circumscribed, possessed.

I suspect that she holds that knowledge — the memory of that one day and night — especially since she is now the sole possessor — as tightly, and securely, as one might clench some bright small gem in one's fist: not a gem given to one by some favored or beloved individual but, even more valuable, some gem found while out on a walk — perhaps by happenstance, or perhaps by some unavoidable rhythm of fate — and hence containing great magic, great strength.

Such is the nature of the kinds of people living, scattered here and there, in this valley.

Swans

I GOT TO KNOW Billy and Amy, over the years, about as well as you get to know anybody up here, which is to say not too well.

They were my nearest neighbors. They saw me fall in and out of love three times, being rejected — abandoned — all three times.

And though that's not the story, they were good neighbors to me then, in those hard days. Amy had been a baker in Chicago, thirty years before, and even after coming out here to be with Billy she'd never stopped baking. She was the best baker who ever lived, I think: huckleberry pies and sweet rolls and the most incredible loaves of bread. I've heard it said that when you die you enter a room of bright light, and that you can smell bread baking just around the corner. I've read accounts of people who've died and come back to life, and their stories are all so similar I believe that's how it is.

And that's what this end of the valley — the south fork of it, rising against the flex of the mountains — smells like all the time, because Amy is almost always baking. The scent of her fresh loaves drifts across the green meadows and hangs along the riverbanks. Sometimes I'll be hiking in the woods, two or three miles up into the mountains, and I'll catch a whiff of bread, and I'll feel certain that she's just taken some out of the oven, miles below. I know that's a long way for a human to catch a scent, but bears can scent food at distances of seven miles, and wolves even farther. Living up here sharpens one's senses. The social senses atrophy a bit, but the wild body becomes stronger. I have seen men here lift the back ends of trucks and roll logs out of the woods that a draft horse couldn't pull. I've seen a child chase down a runaway tractor and catch it from behind, climb up, and turn the ignition off before it went into the river. Several old women up here swim in the river all year round, even through the winter. Dogs live to be twenty, twenty-five years old.

And above it all — especially at this south end of the valley — Amy's bread-scents hang like the smells from heaven's kitchen.

All that rough stuff — the miracle strength, the amazing bodies — that's all fine, but also, we take it for granted; it's simply what the valley brings out, what it *summons*.

But the gentle stuff — that's what I hold in awe; that's what I like to watch.

Gentlest of all were Amy and Billy.

All his life, Billy worked in the woods, sawing down trees on his land in the bottoms, six days a week. He'd take the seventh day off — usually a Sunday — to rest his machinery.

There weren't any churches in the little valley, and if there had been, I don't know if he and Amy would have gone.

Instead, he would take Amy fishing on the Yaak River in their wooden canoe. I'd see them out there on the flats above the falls, fishing with cane poles and crickets for trout — ten- and fifteen-pound speckled beauties with slab bellies that lived in the deepest holes in the stillness up above the falls, waiting to intercept any nymphs that floated slowly past. Those trout were easy to catch, would hit anything that moved. Billy and Amy wore straw hats. The canoe was green. Amy liked to fish. The hot summer days would be *ringing* with stillness, and then when Amy hooked one, it would seem that the whole valley could hear her shout.

The great trout would pull their canoe around on the river, held only by that one thin tight fly-line, spinning their canoe in circles while Amy shrieked and Billy paddled with one hand to stay up with the fish, maneuvering into position so he could try to net it with his free hand — and Amy holding on to that flexing cane pole and hollering.

They were as much a part of the valley, living there in the south fork, as the trees and the river and the very soil itself, as much a part and substance of the valley as the tremulous dusk swamp-cries of the woodcock in summer.

And the swans.

Five of them, silent as gods, lived on a small pond in the woods below Billy and Amy's cabin, gliding in elegant circles and never making a sound. Amy said they never sang like other birds — that they would remain silent all their lives, until they died, at which point they would stretch out their long necks and sing beautifully, and that that was where the phrase "swan song" came from.

And it was for the swans as much as for anyone that Amy baked her bread. She had a park bench at the pond's edge that Billy had made for her, and every evening Amy would take a loaf of bread there and feed it, crumb by crumb, to the beautiful big birds as dusk slid in from out of the trees.

Amy would toss bread crumbs at the black-masked swans until it was dark, until she could see only their ghostly shapes moving pale through the night, the swans lunging at the sound of the bread crumbs hitting the water. I had sat there with her on occasion.

On the very coldest nights — when the swans were able to keep the pond from freezing only by swimming in tight circles in the center, while the shelf-ice kept creeping out, trying to freeze around their feet and lock them up, making them easy prey for coyotes or wolves or foxes — Amy would build warming fires all around the pond's edge. Wilder swans would have moved on, heading south for the hot-springs country around Yellowstone or western Idaho, where they could winter in splendor, as if in a sauna, but these swans had gotten used to Amy's incredible breads, I guess, and also believed — knew — that she would build fires for them if it got too cold.

They weren't tame. She was just a part of their lives. I think she must have seemed as much a natural phenomenon to these swans as the hot springs and geysers must have seemed to other swans, farther south.

From my cabin on the hill, I'd see the glow from Amy's fires begin to flicker through the woods, would see the long tree shadows dancing across the snowfields, firelight back in the timber, and because I was her neighbor, I'd help her build the fires.

Billy would be out there, too, often in his shirtsleeves, no matter how cold the weather. It was known throughout the valley that Billy slept naked with the windows open every night of the year, like an animal, so that it would help him get ready for winter — and he was famous for working shirtless in zero-degree weather, and for ignoring the cold, for liking it, even. It was nothing to see Billy walking down the road in a snowstorm, six miles to the mercantile for a bottle of milk or a beer, wearing only a light jacket and with his hands shoved down in his pockets, bareheaded, ten below, and the snow coming down like it wasn't ever going to stop.

Billy had always been precise — a perfectionist, the only one in the valley — but during this year I am telling about he seemed more that way than ever. Even his body was in perfect shape, like a mountain lion's — a narrow waist but big shoulders and arms from sawing wood endlessly. But there were indications that he was human and not some forever-running animal. He was going bald, though that was no fault of his. He had brown eyes almost like a child's, and a mustache. He still had all of his teeth (except for one gold one in the front), which was unusual for a logger.

He took his various machines apart daily, in the dusty summers, and oiled and cleaned them. I think he liked to do this not just for fanatical maintenance but also to show the machines his control over them; reminding them, perhaps, every evening, that he created them each day when he took them in his hands. That his work gave them their souls — the rumbling saw, the throbbing generator, and his old red logging truck.

Even in the winter, Billy took deep care of his machines, keeping fires going night and day in the wood stoves in his garage, not to warm himself, but to keep the machines "comfortable," he said — to keep the metal from freezing and contracting.

It would make a fine story to tell, a dark and somehow delicious one, to discover at this point that of all the concern and even love that Billy gave to his machines was at a cost, that perhaps it came at Amy's expense.

But that was not the case.

He had a *fullness* to him that we just don't often see. He was loving and gentle with Amy, and I would often marvel, over the years I knew him, at how he always seemed to be thinking of her — of how his movements seemed to be dictated by what might bring her pleasure. And I was struck, too, by the easy way he had of being with her. They seemed fresh together: untouched by the world, and as fresh as that bread.

Billy took caution to cut the lengths of stove wood to fit in Amy's various stoves for her bread-baking. He scanned the woods for dead standing or fallen trees, wood that would have the proper grain and dryness to release good and controlled steady heat — good cooking wood.

In some ways Billy was as much a part of that bread's scent hanging over the south fork as was Amy.

But they were her swans.

So Billy and Amy had a lot of fires: for Amy's baking; for Amy's swans, along the shores of the little pond on the coldest nights; for Billy's machines. Fires in Billy and Amy's cabin, with those windows always open.

They used an incredible volume of wood — more wood cut and burned, perhaps, than by any other two people in the history of the world.

I could step on my porch at almost any hour of the day and hear Billy's old saw buzzing away in the rich bottom, where trees sprouted, grew tall, became old, and fell over; and through their midst, all his life, Billy wielded a giant saw that other men would have had trouble even lifting, much less carrying and using.

He kept the woods down there neat; he cut up nearly all of that which had already fallen and carried it out. You could have picnics or ride bicycles or drive cars into those woods if you so desired, between and among the larger, healthier trees, so free of underbrush and downed trees did he keep it.

But no one ever went there. Things only came out of it.

Stove-sized pieces of wood, for Amy's bread. For the swans' bread. For the scent of the valley. The sound of the saw. Billy's huge, cross-striated chest muscles.

What it was like was a balance; Billy's (and Amy's) life was wedged — as if stuck in a chimney — between rise and fall, growth and rot. He had found some magic seam of life, a stasis in those woods, and as long as he could keep the woods the same, he and Amy would stay the same, as would his love for her — as would her love for him.

I would think — without pity — *If I had done it like him, none of them would ever have left. If I'd given it my all, I could have lodged us, wedged us, into that safe place where neither life nor death can erode a kind of harmony or peace — a spirit — but I wasn't a better man. There goes a better man,* I'd think, when I saw him driving out of the woods and down the road in his old red truck, the truck sunk nearly to the ground with its load of fresh wood. *He gave it his all, and continues to give it his all,* I'd think, *and he's going to make it. They're both going to make it.*

I would feel better to realize that — and to see it.

Somebody in this world has to attain peace, I'd think.

Baking was not all Amy knew how to do. She had gone to a music school in Chicago, had been there on a scholarship to play the piano, but then she'd met Billy, who had driven a trailer load of horses out to sell to a man near Chicago, Amy's uncle.

Amy left her bakery, and she left school, too. For thirty years after that, the only times she ever played the piano were on the irregular visits to friends' houses in town, and once or twice a year when she would go to one of the churches in town, sixty miles away, on a Wednesday, alone before God on a Wednesday afternoon in the spring or in the fall, the church dark and cool and quiet, and she would play there, ignoring the church's organ and playing their piano.

I know that loving a woman isn't about giving her things; I know that's an easy and common mistake for men to make, confusing the two. It is the way of other animals in the wild, animals with strong social bonds, to show affection for their mates by bringing in fresh-killed game — but with men and women it is a little more complex. I have watched Billy and Amy, and have watched my three lovers flee the valley — which is the same thing as fleeing me — and I know the best way for a man to love a woman, or woman to love a man, is not to bring gifts, but to simply understand that other person: to understand as much (and with as much passion and concern) as is possible.

Nonetheless, certain presents can sometimes speak eloquently the language of this understanding, and in the last year before Billy became different, before he began to slip, he bought Amy a piano.

Billy had been cutting trees in secret for her — live trees, some of them, not just the standing or fallen dead ones.

Big, beautiful trees — mixed conifers, immense larch and spruce and fir trees, and ponderosa and white pine.

Not a lot of them — just a few every year — on the far side of the bottoms, his father's land, his cutting-ground — and Billy had been saving that money for years, he told me.

A tree cut for love is not the same as a tree cut for money, or for bread-baking — but even so, Billy said, he didn't like doing it, and after he'd made the finishing cut on each piano-tree — cutting one every two or three months — his secret life —

Billy said he would feel queasy, as if he were sawing off a man's thigh: the forest, and life, growth, that dear and sacred and powerful to him.

It was not that Billy did not understand death — he did. Or said he thought he did, which is, I guess, as close as you can come, until you're there.

Billy knew — he sensed — something was getting out of balance whenever he'd cut one of those ancient trees — but he'd sit and rest after the big tree leaned and then fell, crashing slowly through the leafy canopy below, stripping limbs off other trees, even taking smaller trees with it — shaking the forest when it hit, making the woods jump.

Billy would sit on a log and just breathe, he told me, and think about nothing but love, about Amy, and he would not move, he said, until he felt that balance — that strange stasis — return to the woods.

The way he put it — what he was looking for, sitting there in the woods like that, barely breathing — was that he would wait until the woods "had forgotten him again." Then he would feel safe and free to move back through their midst.

So he knew what he was doing, in this life; it wasn't just by accident that he'd holed up in this valley, wedged between the past and the future. Just him and Amy. He had a good feel for what was going on. The way he worked at sawing those logs every day was exactly the way he felt about preserving and nurturing his love for and his life with Amy, until the way he went at those logs with his saw *became* his love for Amy.

It was easy to picture Billy just sitting there, mopping his balding head, pouring a cup of water from his thermos in the after-silence of each tree felled, and watching, and listening.

Drinking the water in long gulps. A flicker darting through the woods, perhaps, flying from one tree to another, looking for bugs.

Billy's eyes, watching it.

And then home in the evenings, those secret trees resting silent and new-cut, drying out in the forest, and his old red truck laboring, puttering up the hill, past my cabin, home to his wife — past the pond, past Amy in the dusk; Amy seeing the truck pass, waving, throwing a few more bread crumbs to the beautiful, silent, patient swans, and then rising and taking the shortcut through the woods up to their cabin.

The other part of her life. Her husband. She had her swans, and she had a husband. Children? Never. She was suspended as gracefully, as safely, between the past and the future as was Billy.

And then, when Billy had sawed enough logs, he sold them and bought the piano and built a little cabin for her next to the pond, just a tiny cabin which housed only the piano and a bench and a lantern and, of course, a stove. The little piano cabin was full of windows, and Amy would open them if it wasn't raining, and play music to the swans — beautiful classical compositions like Pachelbel's *Canon* and Mozart, but also church music. "Rock of Ages" was one of my favorites, and it carried the farthest. Sometimes I would walk through the woods at dusk and sit on a boulder on the hillside above the river and the pond and listen to the music rising from the trees below.

Other times I'd creep through the woods like an animal to get closer to the pond, and I'd look through the trees and see Amy playing by lantern-light, her face a perfect expression of serenity, playing hard (the thrown-open windows of the little square cabin acting as a giant speaker, so that the sound carried across the hills, up into the mountains, and I liked to think of the mountains absorbing that music, the peace of it settling inches deep into the thin soil, to bedrock, and calming the wild mountains as darkness fell).

Sometimes Amy sang, ever so quietly. It occurred to me as I watched the swans all watch Amy (lined up, floating there on the water like children in a school recital, listening) that Amy had let go of her bakery job, and her music school, as easily as she let go of everything — tossing away all thoughts of controlling the moment (much less the wild future), as if tossing crumbs to the long-necked swans. Casting away all control, and simply being.

Billy had always taught me things. He would stop in and point to my fallen-down wandering fence (I had no livestock, and hence no need of repairing the fence) and tell me that if I'd lay it in a straighter line, that would somehow dissuade the moose from walking through it and knocking it down.

"You can keep those same-sized replacement poles in your barn, too, instead of having to custom cut a new one each time a moose or elk herd walks through," he said, but again, I didn't really care if they knocked it down. I didn't really care if there was a fence or not.

Other times Billy would drive up while I was splitting wood in the side yard and point out that the head of my ax was about to fly off any moment now — that the little splinter-wedge chuck I'd used to wedge it back on the first time was getting loose.

"Soak the handle in salt water," he said. "*Then* drive the wedges in."

Everything could be controlled. I listened to Billy, and nodded, and learned some things, and forgot others.

But in the evenings, I listened to Amy.

I went over to Billy and Amy's for supper about once a month. I felt safe in there, sitting at the kitchen table while Amy baked her tortes, quiches, breads, and pies — showing off, the way a person should probably do from time to time. The kitchen, and perhaps the entire valley, groaned with the bread's scent, which enveloped the deer, the elk, the swans — all living things were aware of it. Yearling wolves fell asleep dreaming of man's heaven, perhaps, not knowing what they were dreaming of, but surely just as at peace as if they had dreamed of their own.

Billy took me out to his barn at our October supper — the moon round and orange, and a breeze from the north — and we walked around in his barn looking at things while Amy baked. Billy had not yet started up the wood stoves in his barn — that would not happen until November or December, when the machines, like the animals, began to get cold. Instead, we just walked around inspecting things. Billy inspected his inventory — the rows of nuts and bolts, oil filters of various shapes and sizes, ignition coils.

Everything gleamed under the light of the shop's lanterns. The concrete floor was spotless, with none of the visceral oil stains one usually sees in such a place. He picked up a set of packed wheel bearings — spun the smooth inside hub like a toy. He had a case of a dozen — a lifetime's supply, perhaps — and when one set went bad, he'd just pull them off and stick in a new set. The bearings glistened with the faintest high-grade condensate of lubrication, of earnest readiness.

"If something happened to me," he said, "you'd take care of her? Not just anybody could take my place. You'd have to learn things she doesn't know, and kind of check in on her. Kind of make sure she had *enough* of everything."

"Nobody could ever take your place, Billy."

"That's what I'm worried about," he said. The big barn was silent except for the flickering hiss of the lanterns: safe and clean and warm, and yet also somehow like a trap.

We blew out the lanterns and went back across the yard (so many stars above!) and into the warm small kitchen. We sat at the table, said grace, and began to eat, closing our eyes in the bliss of the meal. The windows, as ever, were wide open, and the night's cool breezes stirred against our arms and faces as we ate. The wood stove creaked as the fire died down and the cabin cooled.

Night and day; day and night. There is a perfect balance, a drawn and poised moment's tension to everything. Is it peculiarly human, and perhaps evil, to try to hang back — to try to shore up, pause, build a fortress against the inevitable snapping or release of that tension's thread? Of trying to not allow the equation to roll forward, like riffle water over, past, and around the river's boulders?

When things started slipping for Billy, they didn't seem like much, not at first: forgetting names, and forgetting the sequence of things — getting in the truck one morning, he told me, and not remembering to turn the ignition on — putting it in gear, easing the clutch out, and then wondering for several moments why the truck wasn't moving. Those sorts of things were allowed up in this country and were fairly common, though I didn't know why.

Billy was coming by to visit more and more frequently that fall, telling me things out of the blue — giving me knowledge the way someone else might pass out old clothes he no longer had any use for. Maybe Billy knew he was losing the race against rot and was trying to give away as much as he could before it all seeped away. I didn't know that, then. I just listened, and watched, and was glad he was my neighbor.

"You can put sixteen-inch tires on your truck in bad winters," he said. "Gives you another three, four inches clearance. It won't hurt nothin'."

Later in the fall, when the larch needles turned gold and began falling, flying through the air, tiny and slender, covering the road with a soft gold matting, Billy began forgetting to go into the woods.

Instead, he would come over to my place, with his empty truck and his dog, to give me advice, as if to prepare me with what I'd need to know to continue living up here. We'd share a glass of iced tea, and I'd just listen. I could tell he had forgotten my name — the way he looked at me strangely and never used my name anymore. I'd often be wearing my camouflage clothes from having been out in the woods hunting deer, meat for the winter, and sometimes I still had my face painted with charcoal.

Billy would stare at my face for a full minute. His mind was going, gone — over the next ridge — and I wonder what he must have thought, looking at me — wondering if I was a devil, or an angel. I hope that he still recognized me as his neighbor.

"Cut those lodgepole pines behind your house, as soon as they die," he said, "those beetle-killed ones. Get 'em down on the ground where it's damp, so's the eggs can't hatch and spread."

Billy would stare out at my crooked, wandering fences. He'd open his mouth to say something else, but then would close it. We'd be out on my porch.

"Shit. I can't remember what I was going to say." Billy would rub his head, the side of his face. "Shit," he'd sigh, and just sit there — having forgotten, even, that he was on his way to go cut wood.

"Let me take you to a doctor," I said once: a notion as foreign to Billy, surely, as taking him to Jamaica.

"No. No doctors. I've got to pull myself out of this one."

It was exactly like slipping, like walking down a hill pasted with damp yellow aspen and cottonwood leaves in the fall, going down too steep a trail. Your hand reached out and grabbed a tree, and you saved yourself from falling.

His body was still strong — his arms, and his saw-wielding, maul-splitting back as broad as ever — but he was talking slower, and his face looked older, and so did his eyes. They looked — *gentler.*

"Amy," is what he'd say, sometimes, as he looked out at my half-assed fence — unable to remember what it was he wanted to say.

Instead of cutting wood, he'd go back toward his cabin — park on one side of the road, get out, and wander through the woods as if drawn by lodestone (or the smell of the bread) to the pond, where Amy might be sitting on the bench reading, or writing a letter back home, or feeding the eager, expectant swans.

Billy would sit on the bench next to her as he must have when they first met, when they were so raw and unquestionably young and so far from danger.

Amy would come over to my cabin sometimes, on the days that Billy did manage to find his way back into the bottom to cut still more firewood. She was a strong and content and *whole* woman, her own life held together as completely as Billy's, make no mistake about it, and with much more grace, much less muscle — but she was also worried: not for herself, or about being left alone, but for Billy.

There is romantic nonsense these days about the beauty of death, about the terrible end becoming the lovely beginning, and I think that's wrong, a diminution of the beauty of life. Death is as terrible as birth is wonderful. The laws of physics and nature — not romance — dictate this.

It occurs to me that sometimes even nature — raw, silent, solemn, and joyous nature — fears, even if only slightly, rot.

"I'm angry at him," Amy said one day. "He's getting worse." Amy had brought a loaf of bread over and we were sitting on my porch. We could hear Billy's saw running only intermittently — long pauses between work.

"I feel guilty," Amy said. "I feel bad for being angry and afraid. I try to remember all we've had — and all that he's given me — but I can't help it. He's always been the same, and now that he's changing, I'm angry."

"Maybe he will get better," I said lamely.

"He's changing so fast," Amy said. "Never any change before, and now so much of it."

The times when Billy went into the woods to cut logs for all his various fires — the times when he went past my cabin without stopping — he would often miss the turnoff for the small road that went into his woods, and he would just keep going — a mile or two, I suppose. Then I'd hear him stop, and he'd back up the road in reverse, engine groaning — backing all the way to the turnoff — embarrassed, at first, and telling me about it, laughing, on my front porch the next day (as if I'd not been able to see it clearly, with my own eyes, from where I was sitting); but then as it happened more often, he stopped talking about it.

I'd sit there every day and watch him drive past in reverse, backing the big empty truck to a spot where he could turn around and go back into the woods and down onto the land his family had owned for more than a hundred years.

It must have struck some chord in Billy — going backwards like that, with the engine straining, things falling away from him, out the front windshield, getting smaller rather than larger. He took to doing it all the time — driving backwards — even while going to the mercantile for groceries.

It was real hard: watching him whom I admired and respected, whom I wanted to emulate, disappear, as if being claimed by the forest itself.

Other people, however, began to shy away from Billy, in the manner that animals will sometimes avoid another of their kind when it becomes sick.

He no longer seemed to be in that secret seam between wildness and gentleness — the hidden fissure. Amy seemed as safely and permanently ensconced there as ever — but Billy seemed to have suddenly jumped — in the flip of a heartbeat — out to the far end, the very edge of wildness.

I don't mean he was tortured or even unhappy during this last sea change, the fluctuating tremors of the forest claiming him back; if anything, I think there was more sweetness, wildness, and pure joy in it for him than ever — lying there listening to Amy's masterful piano-playing and watching out the open cabin door the ghostly shapes of the swans, watching them as if they had gathered, silently, to watch him.

The great coolness of the net of night, the safety of autumn evenings coming down on them again and again, with the days growing shorter, and less conflict, less ambition, less *trouble* in Billy's mind as the coils and loops and convolutions of his brain smoothed out and erased themselves.

The smell in the valley, as always, of her bread baking.

People in town said that whenever Billy came into the mercantile for groceries, he would walk into the store and just stand there, unable to remember what he had come for.

He would have to borrow the mercantile's radio and call Amy on the shortwave and ask her what it was she needed.

I could see the fright in Billy's eyes, every time I saw him, and in Amy's, too, as the fall progressed and the light snows began.

I remember walking one starry night after the snow was down — early November, and cold — just out walking, going down the road toward town, to the saloon for a beer or two and a breath of fresh air — and Billy's truck came over the hill, sputtering and rattling, from a direction that was away from his cabin. I was glad to see that he was not driving backwards — not at night.

I was a long way past his cabin, a long way up the road. It had been more than an hour since I had gone across the bridge over the little creek by where he lived — the swans paddling in slow circles in the creek, white like ghosts in the moonlight, with the moon's blurry reflection wavering in their ripples, and ice beginning to form on the creek's edges. I imagined that the swans were waiting for Amy's next sonata, these beautiful birds for whom music was an impossibility.

I walked on farther, past the yellow lights of Billy and Amy's cabin, up the hill. I had assumed Billy was at home, that they were both at home, maybe sitting in bed and playing a hand of cards or two before going to sleep, as Amy had told me they often did — playing cards, that is, if Billy could still remember how.

So I was surprised to see him come driving slowly over the hill, his truck slipping on the fresh snow a little; and he stopped, recognizing me in the glare of his headlights — recognizing me, I could tell, but not able to remember my name.

"Hop in, bub," he said. "I was just out looking at things."

I did not believe this was so. I was certain he had forgotten which cabin was his, and I tried to think of a way to tell him when he passed it — wondering if I could say something like, "Is Amy still baking tonight?" and point up the hill toward the yellow squares of light, piecy-looking through the trees.

It was a full moon, and I was surprised to see that Billy was driving with the heater on, and that his windows were rolled up. It was hot and stuffy in the truck. A shooting star streaked in front of us and then disappeared over the trees, and Billy, who was driving with both hands on the wheel, leaning forward and watching the road carefully, looked up at it but said nothing.

Deer kept trotting across the road in front of us, red-eyed in the glare of the headlights — some with antlers, some without — and Billy would turn the lights out immediately whenever he saw a herd of them — in November and December, they were beginning to bunch up and travel together, for protection, and for warmth — and I sat in my seat and gripped the high dashboard, certain that we were going to plow right through the herd.

"What are you doing, Billy?" I said.

He drove intently, slowly, but not slowly enough for my liking. I kept waiting to hear the thud of bodies, and to feel the jolt

— and then when we were past the spot where we should have struck the deer, he would turn the lights back on, and the road in front of us would be empty.

"Sheriff told me to do that," Billy would say each time it happened. "The noise of the truck scares 'em off the road. If you leave the lights on, you blind 'em, and they can't decide which way to go — that's how you end up hittin' 'em — but if you turn your lights off, they can think straight and know to get out of the way."

I had never heard of such a thing and did not believe that he had, either — and it is something that I have never heard of since — but it seemed to give him a distinct pleasure, hunched over the steering wheel and punching the lights off and gliding toward where we had last seen the herd of deer in the middle of the road. He seemed at peace, doing that, and I decided that he was not lost at all, that he just enjoyed getting out and driving at night, and so when we passed the lights of his cabin, I looked up the hill at them but said nothing.

"Take care, Billy," I said when he let me out at my place. It was dark, and I felt that he was frightened of something.

"Take care," he said back to me. "Do you need a light?" he said, rummaging through the toolbox on the seat beside him. "I've got a flashlight, if you need it."

It was only about a ten-yard walk to my cabin.

"No, thanks, I'll be all right. You take care now, Billy."

"You're sure?" he asked.

"I'm sure."

"Take care," he said again. "Take good care."

He drove in a circle in my yard, found the driveway again, and headed up the road toward his house. I stood there and watched him disappear around the bend.

I watched then as Billy's lights came back around the bend — he was driving back to my house in reverse; driving slowly, gears groaning.

Billy backed up in my driveway but didn't get out of his big truck, just leaned out the window. He seemed embarrassed. "Can you show me how to get home?"

He got all the way home in January. He was still trying to cut and load stove wood, as if trying to lay in a hundred years' supply for all of his and Amy's fires, on the day that he did not come back — a short winter's day, as if the apogee of waning light had finally scooped him up, had claimed him.

Amy and I went into the woods with lanterns. A light snow was falling, flakes hissing when they landed on our hot lanterns. Billy was lying on his side in the snow (having shut his saw off, but with his helmet still on), looking as if he had stretched out only to take a nap.

Amy crouched and brushed the snow from his face. There were lengths of firewood scattered all around, wood he had not yet loaded in his truck, but already the snow was covering it.

We lifted him carefully into my truck. I drove, and Amy rode with his head cradled in her lap. She removed his helmet and covered his bare head with her hands as if to keep it warm, or perhaps summon one last surge of force, or even the memory of force.

I glanced at the tall trees above us, tried to guess which ones would be the next to fall, and wondered if the forest felt relieved that Billy was gone now — if those trees would be free now to just rot, once they fell.

We rode past the swans' pond. It was a cold night and earlier in the day Amy had lit a few fires around the edge. The fires were beautiful in the falling snow, though diminished and not putting out much heat. The swans had moved in as close to the small ragged orange fires as they could get without leaving the pond. Their beauty was of no help to them, it seemed; they were cold.

They watched us, silent as ever, as we passed, the swans graceful and perfect in the firelight, and I rolled my window down, thinking that as we passed some of them would cry out at Billy's death. But then I remembered it was only for their own death that they sang, and only that once.

The Prisoners

ARTIE AND DAVE work together. They are going fishing with
Dave's younger brother, Wilson, who has his own company,
even though he is only twenty-eight. He sells and installs cellular
car phones and electronic car locks and things like that.

The three men live in Houston. Wilson is single. Artie and
Dave are not; they are in their late thirties. Artie is still in his
first marriage, though perhaps not for long. Dave is into his second marriage, but it's going well. They both have children:
Artie, two young sons, whom he is not that wild about, and
Dave, two daughters — one with his ex-wife and one with his
new wife.

Dave is wild about both of his daughters, hates to be gone
from either of them for more than a few hours, and each time he
sees them it is like swimming to the surface from a great depth;
when he does not see them, he feels as if his lungs are about to
burst.

Dave's first wife had left him when they had been living in
Orange, New Jersey — had moved to Texas with her boyfriend
and received custody of their daughter two years ago — and so
Dave followed her down to Texas and got a job there, and was
able to see his daughter on Wednesday evenings, plus every
other weekend.

It was in Houston that Dave met and married his new wife,

Nancy, and had the new baby, who to him is just as precious as the first. Because Dave owes his ex-wife $896.12 each month in child support, Dave and Nancy and the baby live in a small apartment in a not-very-safe neighborhood. They can't go for walks at night and, afraid of drive-by shootings, they sleep with lightweight bulletproof flak jackets, with the baby in between them. Dave's learning to be a real estate appraiser, and in his work he has seen how easily bullets can penetrate thin hollow plasterboard walls. He appraised an apartment in Phoenix into which a pistol had been fired, and he was amazed to see that the bullet had traveled through six walls before going through a refrigerator door.

Nancy took six weeks off from her job when the baby was born but has now been back at work for a couple of months. There's a woman they pay over in Bellaire — a forty-minute drive in good traffic, an hour in bad traffic — to watch the baby each day. Under the terms of her maternity leave, Nancy could have taken off eight weeks, but she's heard that her boss rewards employees who come back to work early.

Dave has not been at his job as long as Artie has, but he's better at it, more confident with both people and numbers, and so already he's a little higher in the company than Artie. The boss likes Dave, and likes the way the work isn't the most important thing in the world to Dave. The boss knows that Dave's daughters are what matter to him, and that because of this he doesn't have to worry about his loyalty: knows Dave's not going anywhere. And Dave always gets his work turned in on time; he hasn't been late with a project yet.

Dave is pleasant-looking, tall, friendly, with blue eyes. He smiles a lot, laughs easily, hides from everyone the thing that used to be rage and despair, about his wife taking his daughter away from him, the thing that is now neither rage nor despair, but some harder, sadder, more deadened thing. You couldn't tell that thing was in him unless you cut him open with a knife, or unless he opened up and told you — which he isn't going to do.

Artie is dark, heavy, sulky. He doesn't know how to laugh. He can pretend-laugh, can ridicule things, but he hasn't opened up and laughed, hasn't felt the cleansing opening-up trickling of simple, gurgling laughter since he was about ten or twelve. His skin is as dark as a plum, as if he's bruised. His eyes are hooded from nonspecific worries, from chronic frowning. He's about twenty pounds overweight. When he drinks beer he gets friendlier, though not happier. Artie listens to conservative radio talk shows and feels strongly an impending sense of disaster, as if he is in a fast car that is racing flat-out and hard for a concrete wall. He and Dave and Wilson have taken off a Monday from work to go fishing down near Galveston. They've hired a guide, whom they're supposed to meet at daylight, down at one of the Texas City piers on the Gulf. The guide has said that he will take them to wherever the fish are biting. Artie is worried that they won't catch anything, that the money will be wasted, and on the drive down he keeps pressing Dave and Wilson to reassure him that this is a good guide. Dave and Wilson have been fishing with this guide once before and each caught his limit of speckled trout in only a few hours, though it does not always work out that way, and they tell him this.

Wilson is driving. He's got a new truck with leather seats. He doesn't have a car phone, even though he sells them. He's read that they cause brain cancer, and so instead all he has is a digital pager, which records the number of messages coming into his answering machine back in Houston. Wilson bought a computer program that pointed out to him that, based on last year's data, each incoming phone call brings him — on the average — another $152.18 of business.

The pager is hooked to the sun visor of his truck, and each time it goes off — a rapid series of beeps and clicks — all three men whoop and tally the total: Dave counting with true gusto, elated for his little brother, and Artie sick with green envy but happy at the thought that at least somebody, somewhere, is getting gouged.

It's a lot of work for Wilson to go out and answer each of those calls — to drive out and fix whatever's wrong with the system or to install a new one — but he does it. He has no employees. He's a one-man show. He won't even be twenty-nine for another ten months. It makes him seem richer than he already is, though in his mind, it's a little bit like he's drowning, or gasping for air — like he can't quite get enough air — and he doesn't like that feeling, and he's trying not to worry about the business so much.

Fishing trips, such as this one, with his brother, help.

Even though it is still an hour before daylight, the pager's going off about every ten minutes. If the pager gets too full — it will hold only a certain number of messages, depending on their length — Wilson can stop and get out and make a few calls from a pay phone, but he hopes that doesn't happen today.

As they drive, all Artie talks about — sitting in the back seat and watching the digital glow of the pager, waiting for its red light to blink in the dark, waiting for the beeping to go off again — is his and Dave's work. Even though they saw each other on Friday, they go over it again, shooting the shit about each employee in the office — talking about their work in the familiar but also exploratory manner of raccoons crouched by the side of a creek, fishing for mussels in the night: turning them over with their paws, feeling every ridge, every bump. There is the one who is getting fired, and the one who does not get her reports in on time. There is the good-looking one and the plain one. There is the asshole and the brown-noser, and they laugh and talk about the brown-noser for a while.

Then they talk about the handsome one, whom they dislike intensely because he is arrogant, and finally, after several miles, they settle on the scapegoat, the gullible one, Clifford.

They savage Clifford; it is as if he is meat and they are eating him. It is as if they are cutting him up and swallowing him. Every week there is something new that Clifford's done, or which they've done to Clifford, some small thing to share and to revel over. This morning Artie is telling Dave about how he bad-mouthed Clifford's new truck, a Chevy, as not being nearly as strong as Artie's old truck, a Dodge.

"Oh, he was hot!" Artie hoots. "He started stuttering and saying that all his friends who had horses and who trailered them out to the country each weekend used Chevys, and I interrupted him and said, 'Well, yeah, they're okay trucks for little *weekend* pullers.'" Artie imitates the brush-away hand-waving motion he'd given Clifford — and Dave laughs, too.

"*Weekend* pullers," Dave says. "That's a good one. Him and those damn horses."

Clifford, who is slightly ahead of them in hierarchy, though not a real boss, has been going out to the new racetrack by the airport and has been buying the bargain horses, the ones that are not quite fast enough.

"It's like a compulsion," Artie says. "He's bought about fifty of them so far, and he doesn't show any fucking sign of stopping."

"I could kill him," Dave says, from out of the blue.

Wilson looks at his brother in surprise. Artie laughs a mean laugh.

"I had to go over to his house for a barbecue once, while you were out of town," Dave tells Artie. "Some bullshit office party. He had just been out to the racetrack that day and had brought home two more horses. He had them in his back yard and was feeding them apples and hay and making everyone *touch* them," Dave says. "He kept making everyone pat their flanks, their rumps. *'Feel that,'* he'd say, *'Feel how hard that is.'* I'd never seen such sad pieces of shit in all my life. He says he's going to sell them as polo ponies. He thinks that because they almost ran races, they're some kind of super-horses, and always will be. He thinks almost is real close, instead of real far.

"When he comes in my office to ask me something," Dave goes on, "the first thing I ask him, right away, before he can say anything, is 'How long are you going to be in here?'"

"You tell him that?" Artie says.

"Hell yes," says Dave. "He doesn't like it, but there's nothing he can do. Just because he's above me doesn't mean he can fire me. Besides, he doesn't know shit. He's always asking people to help him fill out his reports. He'll ask the same question five days in a row."

"He does that, doesn't he?" Artie says. "Asks the same question twice." Artie's speaking slowly now, and where before he had a kind of cocksure glittering anger in his dark eyes, doubt is now starting to seep in, and it comes into his voice, too, a change that is so noticeable that Wilson, driving, looks in the rearview mirror to see what's going on.

"Hey, Dave," Artie says — and Wilson recognizes the change-in-voice immediately, recognizes it from his customers:

the bargaining mode, the favor-asking mode. "How do you get all those apartment jobs, now? Apartments are easy. I always get the warehouses," he says.

Dave shrugs. What can he tell Artie? That Artie is raw meat, chum for the company? That his sole purpose for the company, and therefore perhaps in life, is to pull his suit on each morning and hurl his body at the stacks of dull paper, earning his 3 percent, passing on the rest of the bloated profit to the absentee, do-nothing owner of the company, until Artie's body is gray and bent and lifeless and all joy and spontaneity has been sucked from his brain?

Dave shrugs again, looks in the mirror at Artie. Dave heard the waver in Artie's voice, too.

"I just ask for 'em," Dave says, and that is as close to the truth as he wants to come — that he, Dave, gets them, and that Artie does not.

"Warehouses are big," Artie complains. "So fucking big and empty. Nothing in them. A hell of a lot of work," he says. "Shit. Apartments are easy. I could knock out apartments in no time."

"Look," Dave says. He points up the road to a dingy white bus that's traveling the same direction as they are. It's a prison bus from Huntsville: an aging school bus. It's lit up inside with a yellow glow like the light that comes from old bug lamps. Riding through the night like that, it looks as if the prisoners are up on some kind of stage for exhibit, or are floating in light.

The prisoners are jammed shoulder to shoulder, three to a seat, and they are staring straight ahead. Perhaps a hundred of them are packed in there. They are so motionless, so locked into their straight-ahead stares, that it seems certain they must be handcuffed.

There is wire mesh, like a cage, all around the bus's windows, and the bus is moving slowly.

Wilson pulls closer to the bus, on its left, and begins passing it; as he does, the three men are struck by a horrible, giddy kind of silliness. They begin making faces at the prisoners, first Artie and then Dave and then Wilson. They leer and hold their hands up to their ears and pantomime and grin, making taunting gestures of nonsense to the prisoners, and then pass on.

But almost immediately, as if some shell or husk has come back over them, or has instead been peeled back again to reveal who they really are, the three men are a bit remorseful, and embarrassed — a bit shocked — by what they have done. They ride on in silence.

Wilson has switched on the mute button on his pager, but in the darkness, it blinks red again, and Artie utters a quiet "Whoop!"

"Which exit is it?" Wilson asks. "Texas City, or League City?"

"Texas City," Dave says. "I told you that. You'd better slow down and get over. You're going to miss it." Already, there's a lot of traffic, men going to work in the refineries at Baytown, Texas City, and Galveston. The oil comes straight in to the Gulf from the Middle East, from Africa and Russia, from the North Sea, China, and South America, and is refined there on the shore. Refineries and smokestacks line the beach like skyscrapers. The orange and yellow plumes of flare-gas flutter raggedly in the night, but the sight is strangely pretty, oddly comforting. Wilson pulls into the right lane and slows down, watching for the exit. Dave looks back to see where the prison bus is, and he is alarmed to see that it's gaining on them.

"If you speed up and get a ticket," he tells Wilson, "I'll pay for it, as long as you don't let them catch up with us."

Wilson cackles and slows down further.

"I'll get you for this, Wilson," Dave says to his younger brother, and slumps down in his seat. He averts his face as the prison bus passes them once more; but still he cannot help but look.

The driver is giving them a malevolent stare. He's a big man in a uniform, with a crewcut, and for a moment, with his eyes alone, he drills holes in their truck. He's gripping the steering wheel so tightly with his big fists that it seems he will break it off.

"Oh, lovely," Dave says. And is it his imagination, or as the bus passes are all the prisoners on that side of the bus watching out of the corners of their eyes? They are still staring lock-solid straight ahead, as they must have been told to do, but doesn't it seem, too, that there is some hint of peripheral vision, that the prisoners are casting sidelong corner-eyed glances of rage down at them? Memorizing their faces, perhaps, their license plate, their existence, for the prisoners to hold clenched in their hearts for all the rest of their days — gripping that knowledge so tightly until it seems it will crack, and waiting for the day they get out, then, to go looking for them?

And if they do, will they find them? Would they know where to look? Might it be an easy thing for the prisoners to hold on to even a tiny rage for a very long time, given their predicament?

The three men feel strongly that they have made a mistake, in their one errant moment of lightheartedness: some crooked, mistaken flight of frivolousness.

The prison bus gets off ahead of them, at the same exit they're taking.

"Maybe they're all going fishing, too," says Wilson. "Maybe it's like a vacation."

"Maybe they've chartered our same boat," says Artie.

And though none of the men really believes this, there is a long, stultifying tension that builds and builds, as ahead of them, the bus takes the same series of left turns and rights that they are taking, as if it is indeed going out on the pier, too, to meet the guide. And it is finally only at the last intersection that the bus turns right, where Artie and Dave and Wilson are supposed to turn left. Without realizing it, the three men relax and uncoil, and breathe out long, quivery breaths of relief, and then chuckle.

Wilson comes to a full stop before turning left, and the three of them watch the bus, the prisoners bathed in that awful yellow light, travel down the road into the darkness — watching the bus until it is completely gone, tiny red taillights fading into nothing.

The men watch the bus disappear in this manner as if to make themselves believe that it has become nothing, never-was; then, with a glow in the east, they turn toward the sunrise and drive down the pier, along the rock jetty, out to the point where they are to meet their guide.

There is a devastating southwest wind kicking up, one that will muddy the water and make the fishing all but impossible — they will not catch a thing all day — but they do not know this yet, and for the moment it doesn't matter. At the moment, they are still uncoiling, still unwinding, and are driving along in a state of nearly utter peace and freedom, a kind of euphoric silver-heartedness: a clean-breathing, gasping kind of feeling, a good one, which might last for hours.

The Fireman

THEY BOTH STAND ON the other side of the miracle. Their marriage was bad, perhaps even rotting, but then it got better. He — the fireman, Kirby — knows what the reason is: that every time they have an argument, the dispatcher's call sounds, and he must run and disappear into the flames — he is the captain — and while he is gone, his wife, Mary Ann, reorders her priorities, thinks of the children, and worries for him. Her blood cools, as does his. It seems that the dispatcher's call is always saving them. Their marriage settles in and strengthens, afterward, like some healthy, living, supple thing.

She meets him at the door when he returns, kisses him. He is grimy-black, salt-stained and smoky-smelling. They can't even remember what the argument was about. It's almost like a joke, the fact that they were upset about such a small thing — any small thing. He sheds his bunker gear in the utility room and goes straight to the shower. Later, they sit in the den by the fireplace and he drinks a few beers and tells her about the fire. He knows he is lucky — he knows they are both lucky. As long as the city keeps burning, they can avoid becoming weary and numb. Each time he leaves, is drawn away, and then returns to a second chance.

The children — a girl, four, and a boy, two — sleep soundly. It is not so much a city that they live in, but a town —

a suburb on the perimeter of a city in the center of the southern half of the country — a place where it is warm more often than it is cold, so that the residents are not overly familiar with fires: the way a fire spreads from room to room; the way it takes only one small, errant thing in a house to invalidate and erase the whole structure — to bring it all down to ashes and send the building's former occupants out wandering lost and adrift into the night, poorly dressed and without direction.

They often talk until dawn, if the fire has occurred at night. She is his second wife; he is her first husband. Because they are in an unincorporated suburb, his is a volunteer department. Kirby's crew has a station with new equipment — all they could ask for — but there are no salaries, and he likes it that way; it keeps things purer. He has a day job as a computer programmer for an engineering firm that designs steel girders and columns used in industrial construction: warehouses, mills, and factories. The job means nothing to him — he slips along through the long hours of it with neither excitement nor despair, his pulse never rising, and when it is over each day he says goodbye to his coworkers and leaves the office without even the faintest echo of his work lingering in his blood. He leaves it all the way behind, or lets it pass through him like some harmless silver laxative.

But after a fire — holding a can of cold beer, and sitting there next to the hearth, scrubbed clean, talking to Mary Ann, telling her what it had been like, what the cause had been, and who among his men had performed well and who had not — his eyes water with pleasure at his knowing how lucky he is to be getting a second chance with each and every fire.

He would never say anything bad about his first wife, Rhonda — and indeed, perhaps there is nothing bad to say, no failing in which they were not both complicit. It almost doesn't matter; it's almost water under the bridge.

The two children are asleep in their rooms, the swing set and jungle gym out in the back yard. The security of love and constancy — the *safety*. Mary Ann leads the children's choir in church and is as respected for her work with the children as Kirby is for his work with the fires.

It would seem like a fairy-tale story: a happy marriage, one that turned its deadly familiar course around early on, that day six years ago when he signed up to be a volunteer for the fire department. One of those rare marriages, as rare as a jewel or a forest, that was saved by a combination of inner strength and the grace and luck of fortuitous external circumstances — *the world afire*. Who, given the chance, would not choose to leap across that chasm between a marriage that is heading toward numbness and tiredness and one that is instead strengthened, made more secure daily for its journey into the future?

And yet — even on the other side of the miracle, even on the other side of luck — a thing has been left behind: his oldest daughter, his only child from his first marriage, Jenna. She's ten, almost eleven.

There is always excitement and mystery on a fire call. It's as if these things are held in solution just beneath the skin of the earth and are then released by the flames, as if the surface of the world is some errant, artificial crust — almost like a scab — and that there are rivers of blood below, and rivers of fire, rivers of the way things used to be and might some day be again — true but mysterious, and full of power.

It does funny things to people — a fire, that burning away of the thin crust. Kirby tells Mary Ann about two young men in their thirties — lovers, he thinks — who, bewildered and bereft as their house burned, went out into the front yard and began cooking hamburgers for the firefighters as the building burned down.

He tells her about a house full of antiques that could not be salvaged. The attack crew was fighting the fire hard, deep in the building's interior — the building "fully involved" as they say when the wood becomes flame, air becomes flame, world becomes flame. It is the thing the younger firemen live for — not a smoke alarm, lost kitten, or piddly grass fire, but the real thing, a fully involved structure fire — and even the older firemen's hearts are lifted by the sight of one. Even those who have been thinking of retiring (at thirty-seven, Kirby is the oldest man on the force) are made new again by the sight of it, and by the radiant heat, which curls and browns and sometimes even ignites the oak leaves of trees across the street from the fire. The paint of cars parked too close to the fire sometimes begins to blaze spontaneously, making it look as if the cars are traveling very fast.

Bats, which have been out hunting, begin to return in swarms, dancing above the flames, and begin flying in dark, agitated funnels back down into the chimney of a house that's on fire, if it is not a winter fire — if the chimney has been dormant — trying to rescue their flightless young, which are roosting in the chimney, or sometimes the attic, or beneath the eaves. The bats return to the house as it burns down, but no one ever sees any of them come back out. People stand around on the street — their faces orange in the firelight — and marvel, hypnotized at the sight of it, not understanding what is going on with the bats, or any of it, and drawn, too, like somnambulists, to the scent of those blood-rivers, those vapors of new birth that are beginning already to leak back into the world as that skin, that crust, is burned away.

The fires almost always happen at night.

This fire that Kirby is telling Mary Ann about — the one in which the house full of antiques was being lost — was one of the great fires of the year. The men work in teams, as partners — always within sight, or one arm's length contact, of one another, so that one can help the other if trouble is encountered: if the foundation gives way, or a burning beam crashes across the back of one of the two partners, who are not always men; more and more women are volunteering, though none has yet joined Kirby's crew. He welcomes them; of the multiple-alarm fires he's fought with other crews in which there were women firefighters, the women tended to try to out-think rather than out-muscle the fire, which is almost always the best approach.

Kirby's partner now is a young man, Grady, just out of college. Kirby likes to use his intelligence when he fights a fire, rather than just hurling himself at it and risking getting sucked too quickly into its maw and becoming trapped — not just dying himself, but possibly causing harm or death to those members of his crew who might then try to save him — and for this reason Kirby likes to pair himself with the youngest, rawest, most adrenaline-rich trainees entrusted to his care — to act as an anchor of caution upon them, to counsel prudence and moderation even as the world burns down around them.

At the fire in the house of antiques, Kirby and Grady had just come out to rest and to change oxygen tanks. The homeowner had at first been beside himself, shouting and trying to get back into his house, so that the fire marshal had had to restrain him — they had bound him to a tree with a canvas strap

— but now the homeowner was watching the flames almost as if hypnotized. Kirby and Grady were so touched by his change in demeanor — the man wasn't struggling any longer, was instead only leaning out slightly away from the tree, like the masthead on a ship's prow, and sagging slightly — that they cut him loose so that he could watch the spectacle in freedom, unencumbered.

He made no more moves to reenter his burning house, only stood there with watery eyes — whether tears of anguish, or irritation from the smoke, they could not tell — and, taking pity, Kirby and Grady put on new oxygen tanks, gulped down some water, and, although they were supposed to rest, went back into the burning building and began carrying out those pieces of furniture that had not yet ignited, and sometimes even those that had — burning breakfronts, flaming rolltop desks — and dropped them into the man's back yard swimming pool for safekeeping, as the tall trees in the yard crackled and flamed like giant candles, and floating embers drifted down, scorching whatever they touched. Neighbors all around them climbed up onto their cedar-shingled roofs in their pajamas and with garden hoses began wetting down their own roofs, trying to keep the conflagration from spreading.

The business of it has made Kirby neat and precise. He and Grady crouched and lowered the dining room set carefully into the deep end (even as some of the pieces of furniture were still flickering with flame), releasing them to sink slowly, carefully, to the bottom, settling in roughly the same manner and arrangement in which they had been positioned back in the burning house.

There is no room for excess, unpredictability, or recklessness; these extravagances cannot be borne, and Kirby wants

Grady to see and understand this, the sooner the better. The fire hoses must always be coiled in the same pattern, so that when unrolled the male nipple is always nearest the truck and the female farthest away. The backup generators must always have fresh oil and gas in them and be kept in working order; the spanner wrenches must always hang in the same place.

The days go by in long stretches, twenty-three and a half hours at a time, but in the last half-hour, in the moment of fire, when all the old rules melt down and the new world becomes flame, the importance of a moment, of a second, is magnified ten-thousand-fold — is magnified to almost an eternity, and there is no room for even a single mistake. Time inflates to a greater density than iron. You've got to be able to go through the last half-hour, that wall of flame, on instinct alone, or by force of habit, by rote, by feel.

An interesting phenomenon happens when time catches on fire like this. It happens even to the veteran firefighters. A form of tunnel vision develops — the heart pounding almost two hundred times a minute and the pupils contracting so tightly that vision almost vanishes. The field of view becomes reduced to an area about the size of another man's helmet, or face: his partner, either in front of or behind him. If the men ever become separated by sight or sound, they are supposed to freeze instantly and then begin swinging their pikestaff, or a free arm, in all directions, and if their partner does the same, is within one or even two arms' lengths, their arms will bump each other and they can continue — they can rejoin the fight, as the walls flame vertically and the ceiling and floors melt and fall away.

The firefighters carry motion sensors on their hips, which send out piercing electronic shrieks if the men stop moving for more than thirty seconds. If one of those goes off, it means that a firefighter is down — that he has fallen and injured himself or has passed out from smoke inhalation — and all the firefighters stop what they are doing and turn and converge on the sound, if possible, centering back to it like the bats pouring back down the chimney.

A person's breathing accelerates inside a burning house, and the blood heats, as if in a purge. The mind fills with a strange music. Sense of feel, and memory of how things *ought* to be, becomes everything; it seems that even through the ponderous, fire-resistant gloves the firefighters could read Braille if they had to. As if the essence of all objects exudes a certain clarity, just before igniting.

Everything in its place; the threads, the grain of the canvas weave of the fire hoses tapers back toward the male nipples; if lost in a house fire, you can crouch on the floor and with your bare hand — or perhaps even through the thickness of your glove, in that hyper-tactile state — follow the hose back to its source, back outside, to the beginning.

The ears — the lobes of the ear, specifically — are the most temperature-sensitive part of the body. Many times the heat is so intense that the firefighters' suits begin smoking and their helmets begin melting, while deep within the firefighters are still insulated and protected: but they are taught that if the lobes of their ears begin to feel hot, they are to get out of the building immediately, that they themselves may be about to ignite.

It's intoxicating; it's addictive as hell.

The fire does strange things to people. Kirby tells Mary Ann that it's usually the men who melt down first — they seem to lose their reason sooner than the women. That particular fire in which they sank all the man's prize antiques in the swimming pool, after the man was released from the tree (the top of which was flaming, dropping ember-leaves into the yard, and even onto his shoulders, like fiery moths), he walked around into the back yard and stood next to his pool, with his back turned toward the burning house, and began busying himself with his long-handled dip net, laboriously skimming — or endeavoring to skim — the ashes from the pool's surface.

Another time — a fire in broad daylight — a man walked out of his burning house and went straight to his greenhouse, which he kept filled with flowering plants for his twenty or more hummingbirds of various species. He was afraid that the fire would spread to the greenhouse and burn up the birds, so he closed himself in there and began spraying the birds down with the hose, as they flitted and whirled from him, and he kept spraying them, trying to keep their brightly colored wings wet so they would not catch fire.

Kirby tells Mary Ann all of these stories — a new one each time he returns — and they lie together on the couch until dawn. The youngest baby, the boy, has just given up nursing; Kirby and Mary Ann are just beginning to earn back moments of time together — little five- and ten-minute wedges of time — and Mary Ann naps with her head on his fresh-showered shoulder, though in close like that, at the skin level, she can still smell the charcoal, can taste it. Kirby has scars across his neck and back, pockmarks where embers have landed and burned through his suit, and she, like the children, likes to touch these; the small, slick feel of them is like smooth stones from a river. Kirby earns several each year, and he says that before it is over he will look like a Dalmatian. She does not ask him what he means by "when it is all over," and she holds back, reins herself back, to keep from asking the question, "When will you stop?"

Everyone has fire stories. Mary Ann's is that when she was

a child she went into the bathroom at her grandmother's house, took off her robe, laid it over the plug-in portable electric heater, and sat on the commode. The robe quickly leapt into flame, and the peeling old wallpaper caught on fire, too — so much flame that she could not get past — and she remembers even now, twenty-five years later, how her father had had to come in and lift her up and carry her back out — and how that fire was quickly, easily extinguished.

But that was a long time ago and she has her own life, needs no one to carry her in or out of anywhere. All that has gone away, vanished; her views of fire are not a child's but an adult's. Mary Ann's fire story is tame, it seems, compared to the rest of the world's.

She counts the slick small oval scars on his back: twenty-two of them, like a pox. She knows he is needed. He seems to thrive on it. She remembers both the terror and the euphoria after her father whisked her out of the bathroom, as she looked back at it — at the dancing flames she had birthed. Is there greater power in lighting a fire or in putting one out?

He sleeps contentedly there on the couch. She will not ask him — not yet. She will hold it in for as long as she can, and watch — some part of her desirous of his stopping, but another part not.

She feels as she imagines the street-side spectators must, or even the victims of the fires themselves, the homeowners and renters: a little hypnotized, a little transfixed, and there is a confusion, as if she could not tell you nor her children — could not be sure — whether she was watching him burn down to the ground or watching him being born and built up, standing among the flames like iron being cast from the earth.

She sleeps, her fingers light across his back. She dreams the twenty-two scars are a constellation in the night. She dreams that the more fires he fights, the safer and stronger their life becomes.

She wants him to stop. She wants him to go on.

They awaken on the couch at dawn to the baby's murmurings from the other room and the four-year-old's — the girl's — soft sleep-breathings. The sun, orange already, rising above the city. Kirby gets up and dresses for work. He could do it in his sleep. It means nothing to him. It is its own form of sleep, and these moments on the couch, and in the shells of the flaming buildings, are their own form of wakefulness.

Some nights, he goes over to Jenna's house — to the house of his ex-wife. No one knows he does this: not Mary Ann, and not his ex-wife, Rhonda, and certainly not Jenna — not unless she knows it in her sleep and in her dreams, which he hopes she does.

He wants to breathe her air; he wants her to breathe his. It is a biological need. He climbs up on the roof and leans over the chimney, and listens — *silence* — and inhales, and exhales.

The fires usually come about once a week. The time between them is peaceful at first but then increasingly restless, until finally the dispatcher's radio sounds in the night and Kirby is released. He leaps out of bed — he lives four blocks from the station — kisses Mary Ann, kisses his daughter and son sleeping in their beds, and then is out into the night, hurrying but not running across the lawn. He will be the first one there, or among the first — other than the young firemen who may already be hanging out at the station, watching movies and playing cards, just waiting.

Kirby gets in his car — the chief's car — and cruises the neighborhood slowly, savoring his approach. There's no need to rush and get to the station five or ten seconds sooner, when he'll have to wait another minute or two anyway for the other firemen to arrive.

It takes him only five seconds to slip on his bunker gear, ten seconds to start the truck and get it out of the driveway.

There used to be such anxiety, getting to a fire: the tunnel vision beginning to constrict from the very moment he heard the dispatcher's voice. But now he knows how to save it, how to hold it at bay — that powerhousing of the heart, which now does not kick into life, does not come into being, until the moment Kirby comes around the corner and first sees the flames.

In her bed — in their bed — Mary Ann hears and feels the rumble of the big trucks leaving the station; hears and feels in her bones the belch of the air horns, and then the going-away sirens. She listens to the dispatcher's radio — hoping it will remain silent after the first call, will not crackle again, calling more and more stations to the blaze. Hoping it will be a small fire, and containable.

She lies there, warm and in love with her life — with the blessing of her two children asleep there in her own house, in the other room, safe and asleep — and she tries to imagine the future, tries to picture being sixty years old, seventy, and then eighty. How long — and of that space or distance ahead, what lies within it?

Kirby gets her — Jenna — on Wednesday nights and on every other weekend. On the weekends, if the weather is good, he sometimes takes her camping and lets the assistant chief cover for him. Kirby and Jenna cook over an open fire; they roast marshmallows. They sleep in sleeping bags in a meadow beneath stars. When he was a child Kirby used to camp in this meadow with his father and grandfather, and there would be lightning bugs at night, but those are gone now.

On Wednesday nights — Kirby has to have her back at Rhonda's by ten — they cook hamburgers, Jenna's favorite food, on the grill in the back yard. This one constancy — this one small sacrament. The diminishment of their lives shames him — especially for her, she for whom the whole world should be widening and opening, rather than constricting already.

She plays with the other children, the little children, afterward, all of them keeping one eye on the clock. She is quiet, inordinately so — thrilled just to be in the presence of her father, beneath his huge shadow; she smiles shyly whenever she notices that he is watching her. And how can she not be wondering why it is, when it's time to leave, that the other two children get to stay?

He drives her home cheerfully, steadfastly, refusing to let her see or even sense his despair. He walks her up the sidewalk to Rhonda's like a guest. He does not go inside.

By Saturday — if it is the off-weekend in which he does not have her — he is up on the roof again, trying to catch the scent of her from the chimney; sometimes he falls asleep up there, in a brief catnap, as if watching over her and standing guard.

A million times he plays it over in his mind. Could I have saved the marriage? Did I give it absolutely every last ounce of effort? Could I have saved it?

No. Maybe. *No.*

It takes a long time to get used to the fires; it takes the young firemen, the beginners, a long time to understand what is required: that they must suit up and walk right into a burning house.

They make mistakes. They panic, breathe too fast, and use up their oxygen. It takes a long time. It takes a long time before they calm down and meet the fires on their own terms, and the fires'.

In the beginning, they all want to be heroes. Even before they enter their first fire, they will have secretly placed their helmets in the ovens at home to soften them up a bit — to dull and char and melt them slightly, so anxious are they for combat and its validations: its contract with their spirit. Kirby remembers the first house fire he entered — his initial reaction was "You mean I'm going in *that?*" — but enter it he did, fighting it from the inside out with huge volumes of water — the water sometimes doing as much damage as the fire — his new shiny suit yellow and clean amongst the work-darkened suits of the veterans.

Kirby tells Mary Ann that after that fire he drove out into the country and set a little grass fire, a little pissant one that was in no danger of spreading, then put on his bunker gear and spent all afternoon walking around in it, dirtying his suit to just the right color of anonymity.

You always make mistakes, in the beginning. You can only hope that they are small or insignificant enough to carry little if any price: that they harm no one. Kirby tells Mary Ann that on one of his earliest house fires, he was riding in one of the back seats of the fire engine facing backwards. He was already packed up — bunker gear, air mask, and scuba tank — so that he couldn't hear or see well, and he was nervous as hell. When they got to the house that was on fire — a fully involved, "working" fire — the truck screeched to a stop across the street from it. The captain leapt out and yelled to Kirby that the house across the street was on fire.

Kirby could see the flames coming out of the first house, but he took the captain's orders to mean that it was the house across the street from the house on fire that he wanted Kirby to attack — that it too must be burning — and so while the main crew thrust itself into the first burning house, laying out attack lines and hoses and running up the hook-and-ladder, Kirby fastened his own hose to the other side of the truck and went storming across the yard and into the house across the street.

He assumed there was no one in it, but as he turned the knob on the front door and shoved his weight against it, the two women who lived inside opened it so that he fell inside, knocking one of them over and landing on her.

Kirby tells Mary Ann that it was the worst he ever got the tunnel vision, that it was like running along a tightrope — that it was almost like being blind. They are on the couch again, in the hours before dawn; she's laughing. Kirby couldn't see flames anywhere, he tells her — his vision reduced to a space about the size of a pinhead — so he assumed the fire was up in the attic. He was confused as to why his partner was not yet there to help him haul his hose up the stairs. Kirby says that the women were protesting, asking why he was bringing the hose into their house. He did not want to have to take the time to explain to them that the most efficient way to fight a fire is from the inside out. He told them to just be quiet and help him pull. This made them so angry that they pulled extra hard — so hard that Kirby, straining at the top of the stairs now, was bowled over again.

When he opened the attic door, he saw that there were no flames. There was a dusty window in the attic, and out it he could see the flames of the house across the street, really rocking now, going under. Kirby says that he stared at it a moment and then asked the ladies if there was a fire anywhere in their house. They replied angrily that there was not.

He had to roll the hose back up — he left sooty hose marks and footprints all over the carpet — and by this time the house across the street was so engulfed and Kirby was in so great a hurry to reach it that he began to hyperventilate, and he blacked out, there in the living room of the nonburning house.

He got better, of course — learned his craft better — learned it well, in time. No one was hurt. But there is still a clumsiness in his heart, in all of their hearts — the echo and memory of it — that is not that distant. They're all just fuckups, like anyone else, even in their uniforms: even in their fire-resistant gear. You can bet that any of them who come to rescue you or your home have problems that are at least as large as yours. You can count on that. There are no real rescuers.

Kirby tells her about what he thinks was his best moment — his moment of utter, breathtaking, thanks-giving luck. It happened when he was still a lieutenant, leading his men into an apartment fire. Apartments were the worst, because of the confusion; there was always a greater risk of losing an occupant in an apartment fire, simply because there were so many of them. The awe and mystery of making a rescue — the holiness of it, like a birth — in no way balances the despair of finding an occupant who's already died, a smoke or burn victim — and if that victim is a child, the firefighter is never the same and almost always has to retire after that; his or her marriage goes bad, and life is never the same, never has deep joy and wonder to it again.

The men and women spend all their time and energy fighting the enemy, *fire* — fighting the way it consumes structures, consumes air, consumes darkness — but then when it takes a life, it is as if some threshold has been crossed. It is for the firemen who discover that victim a feeling like falling down an elevator shaft, and there is sometimes guilt, too, that the thing they were so passionate about, fighting fire — a thing that could be said to bring them relief, if not pleasure — should have this as one of its costs.

They curse stupidity, curse mankind, when they find a victim, and are almost forever after brittle.

This fire, the apartment fire, had no loss of occupants, no casualties. It was fully involved by the time Kirby got his men into the structure, Christmas Eve, and they were doing room-to-room searches. No one ever knows how many people live in an apartment complex: how many men, women, and children, coming and going. They had to check every room.

Smoke detectors — thank God! — were squalling everywhere, though that only confused the men further — the sound slightly less piercing, but similar, to the motion sensors on their hip belts, so that they were constantly looking around in the smoke and heat to be sure that they were all still together, partner with partner.

Part of the crew fought the blazes, while the others made searches: horrible searches, for many of the rooms were burning so intensely that if anyone was still inside it would be too late to do anything for them.

If you get trapped by the flames, you can activate your ceased-motion sensor. You can jab a hole in the fire hose at your feet. The water will spew up from the hose, spraying out of the knife hole, like an umbrella of steam and moisture — a water shield, which will buy you ten or fifteen more seconds. You crouch low, sucking on your scuba gear, and wait, if you can't get out. They'll come and get you if they can.

This fire — the one with no casualties — had all the men stumbling with tunnel vision. There was something different about this fire — they would talk about it afterward — it was almost as if the fire wanted them, had laid a trap for them.

They were all stumbling and clumsy, but still they checked the rooms. Loose electrical wires dangled from the burning walls and from crumbling, flaming ceilings. The power had been shut off, but it was every firefighter's fear that some passerby, well meaning, would see the breakers thrown and would flip them back on, unthinking.

The hanging, sagging wires trailed over the backs of the men like tentacles as they passed beneath them. The men blew out walls with their pickaxes, ventilated the ceilings with savage maulings from their lances. Trying to sense, to *feel,* amidst the confusion, where someone might be — a survivor — if anyone was left.

Kirby and his partner went into the downstairs apartment of a trophy big game hunter. It was a large apartment and on the walls were the stuffed heads of various animals from all over the world. Some of the heads were already ablaze — flaming rhinos, burning gazelles — and as Kirby and his partner entered, boxes of ammunition began to go off: shotgun shells and rifle bullets, whole caseloads of them. Shots were flying in all directions, and Kirby made the decision right then to pull his men from the fire.

In thirty seconds he had them out — still the fusillade continued — and thirty seconds after that the whole second floor collapsed: an inch-and-a-half-thick flooring of solid concrete dropped like a fallen cake down to the first floor, crushing the space where the men had been half a minute earlier, the building folding in on itself and being swallowed by itself, by its fire.

There was a grand piano in the lobby and somehow it was not entirely obliterated when the ceiling fell, so that a few crooked, clanging tunes issued forth as the rubble shifted, settled, and burned: and still the shots kept firing.

No casualties. All of them went home to their families that night.

One year Rhonda tells Kirby that she is going to Paris with her new fiancé for two weeks and asks if Kirby can keep Jenna. His eyes sting with happiness. Two weeks of clean air, a gift from out of nowhere. A thing that was his and taken away, now brought back. *This must be what it feels like to be rescued,* he thinks.

Mary Ann thinks often of how hard it is for him — she thinks of it almost every time she sees him with Jenna, reading to her, or helping her with something — and they discuss it often, but even at that, even in Mary Ann's great lovingness, she underestimates it. She thinks she wants to know the full weight of it, but she has no true idea. It transcends words — spills over into his actions — and still she, Mary Ann, cannot know the whole of it.

Kirby dreams ahead to when Jenna is eighteen; he dreams of reuniting. He continues to take catnaps on the roof by her chimney. The separation from her betrays and belies his training; it is greater than an arm's length distance.

The counselors tell him never to let Jenna see this franticness — this gutted, hollow, gasping feeling.

As if wearing blinders — unsure of whether the counselors are right or not — he does as they suggest. He thinks that they are probably right. He knows the horrible dangers of panic.

And in the meantime, the marriage strengthens, becomes

more resilient than ever. Arguments cease to be even arguments, anymore, merely differences of opinion; the marriage is reinforced by the innumerable fires and by the weave of his comings and goings. It becomes a marriage as strong as a galloping horse. His frantic attempts to keep drawing clean air are good for the body of the marriage.

Mary Ann worries about the fifteen or twenty years she's heard get cut off the back end of all firefighters' lives: all those years of sucking in chemicals — burning rags, burning asbestos, burning formaldehyde — but still she does not ask him to stop.

The cinders continuing to fall across his back like meteors; twenty-four scars, twenty-five, twenty-six. She knows she could lose him. But she knows he will be lost for sure without the fires.

She prays in church for his safety. Sometimes she forgets to listen to the service and instead gets lost in her prayers. It's as if she's being led out of a burning building herself; as if she's trying to remain calm, as someone — her rescuer, perhaps — has instructed her to do.

She forgets to listen to the service. She finds herself instead thinking of the secrets he has told her: the things she knows about fires that no one else around her knows.

The way light bulbs melt and lean or point toward a fire's origin — the gases in incandescent bulbs seeking, sensing that heat, so that you can often use them to tell where a fire started: the direction in which the light bulbs first began to lean.

A baby is getting baptized up at the altar, but Mary Ann is still in some other zone — she's still praying for Kirby's safety, his survival. The water being sprinkled on the baby's head reminds her of the men's water shields: of the umbrella-mist of spray that buys them extra time.

As he travels through town to and from his day job, he begins to define the space around him by the fires that have visited it, which he has engaged and battled. *I rescued that one, there, and that one*, he thinks. *That one*. The city becomes a tapestry, a weave of that which he has saved and that which he has not — with the rest of the city becoming simply all that which is between points, waiting to burn.

He glides through his work at the office. If he were hollow inside, the work would suck something out of him — but he is not hollow, only asleep or resting, like some cast-iron statue from the century before. Whole days pass without his being able to account for them. Sometimes at night, lying there with Mary Ann — both of them listening for the dispatcher — he cannot recall whether he even went into the office that day or not.

He wonders what she is doing: what she is dreaming of. He rises and goes in to check on their children — to simply look at them.

When you rescue a person from a burning building, the strength of their terror is unimaginable: it is enough to bend iron bars. The smallest, weakest person can strangle and overwhelm the strongest. There is a drill that the firemen go through, on their hook-and-ladder trucks — mock-rescuing someone from a window ledge, or the top of a burning building. Kirby picks the strongest fireman to go up on the ladder, and then demonstrates how easily he can make the fireman — vulnerable, up on that ladder — lose his balance. It's always staged, of course — the fireman is roped to the ladder for safety — but it makes a somber impression on the young recruits watching from below: the big man being pushed backwards by one foot, or one hand, falling and dangling by the rope: the rescuer suddenly in need of rescuing.

You can see it in their eyes, Kirby tells them — speaking of those who panic. You can see them getting all wall-eyed. The victims-to-be look almost normal, but then their eyes start to cross, just a little. It's as if they're generating such strength within — such *torque* — that it's causing their eyes to act weird. So much torque that it seems they'll snap in half — or snap you in half, if you get too close to them.

Kirby counsels distance to the younger firemen. Let the victims climb onto the ladder by themselves, when they're like that. Don't let them touch you. They'll break you in half. You can see the torque in their eyes.

Mary Ann knows all this. She knows it will always be this way for him — but she does not draw back. Twenty-seven scars, twenty-eight. He does not snap; he becomes stronger. She'll never know what it's like, and for that she's glad.

Many nights he runs a fever for no apparent reason. Some nights, it is his radiant heat that awakens her. She wonders what it will be like when he is too old to go out on the fires. She wonders if she and he can survive that: the not-going.

There are days when he does not work at his computer. He turns the screen on but then goes over to the window for hours at a time and turns his back on the computer. He's up on the twentieth floor. He watches the flat horizon for smoke. The wind gives a slight sway, a slight tremor to the building.

Sometimes — if he has not been to a fire recently enough — Kirby imagines that the soles of his feet are getting hot. He allows himself to consider this sensation — he does not tune it out.

He stands motionless — still watching the horizon, looking and hoping for smoke — and feels himself igniting, but makes no movement to still or stop the flames. He simply burns, and keeps breathing in, detached, as if it is some structure other than his own that is aflame and vanishing, as if he can keep the two separate — his good life, and the other one, the one he left behind.

The Cave

RUSSELL HAD QUIT HIS job as a coal miner on his twenty-fifth birthday, though still, five years later, he would occasionally spray flecks of blood when he coughed. But he was as big as a horse, and to look at him no one would ever have guessed that he was not completely healthy.

Sissy knew it, as they had had numerous conversations, increasingly intimate, on their lunch and dinner dates during the last month, though she was keenly aware that there was much about him that she did not know, too. They were traveling a full day's journey from Mississippi to West Virginia to visit the country where Russell had once worked and to go canoeing there.

Sissy was both excited and nervous; they had left Mississippi long before the sun had risen, and all day she had been filled with the feeling that the day was like a present that was waiting to be unwrapped.

By early afternoon they had passed through Alabama and were up into the foothills of the Appalachians. They drove deeper into the mountains: up craggy canyons and down shady hollows, as if disappearing into the folds of the earth. They passed the leached-out brushfields of revegetated strip mines, as well as the slaughterous new ruins of ongoing ones: big trucks hauling out load after load, pouring out rivers of black diesel smoke from their riddled tailpipes as they thundered wildly down the twisted mountains and then groaned and growled slowly back up the hills.

They got caught behind one such slow-moving caravan, and rather than fight it they pulled over and went for a short walk into the woods. Russell could feel a cool breeze moving through the old forest, and he said that on that breeze he could detect the odors of an abandoned mine.

Sissy did not believe him but went with him looking for it, watching him work into the breeze like a hound, casting laterally until the scent disappeared and then changing directions and casting forward in the opposite direction, zeroing in on whatever odor he was able to discern from all others. Sissy could detect only a faint coolness, no scent, but Russell led them right up to the lip of the old adit, and they stood before it, not seeing it at first, for brush had grown over the opening.

Russell crouched down and parted the leaves, and Sissy saw the dark opening, scarcely wider than a man's body. She leaned in and felt the breeze issuing from it, cool now against her sweaty face. The mine's breath stirred the damp tendrils of her hair and carried the faintest hints of sulfur. She wondered if old rocks smelled different from new rocks — as if such things might have changed slightly in the last several hundred million years. She thought possibly she could smell the faintest odor of men, too, and wondered how recently or distantly they might have abandoned this place.

Emerald-bright moss grew around the hole; wild violets formed scattered bouquets, as if someone, or something, had been buried below and was being honored.

"How far down does it go?" Sissy asked.

Russell lay down on his belly and examined the hole. It was

barely wider than his shoulders. A yellow butterfly drifted past his face. "There are rungs still hammered into the walls," he said. "We could climb down and see."

"Do you think it has a bottom?"

"It has to have a bottom," he said.

"You go first," Sissy said. "What do I do if you fall?"

"Crawl back out, and wait for me to climb up," Russell said.

"Will it be cold or hot down there?" Sissy asked. Russell didn't answer; he was already lowering himself into the hole. It was a tight squeeze and his hips would not quite fit, so that he was stuck already, half in the earth and half out. He strained there for a moment, then wriggled back out.

"Do you mind if I undress?" he asked.

"No," said Sissy, and watched as he kicked off his shoes and pulled off his shirt, heavy denim jeans, and finally his underwear.

"Tell me why I should go down here with you?" said Sissy.

"You don't have to," he said, easing into the hole.

She paused, then looked around before slipping out of her own clothes — paused again with her bra and underwear, shock white — the light coming down through the green dappling of leaves felt warmer, different, on her bare skin — and then she slipped out of those as well, folded her clothes neatly next to his rumpled pile, and descended.

"You blocked out the light," he said, from ten feet below.

She looked up. "It's still there," she said.

The adit was cool and slick with spring-trickle. The limestone walls were smoothed with years of water-seep, and they felt good against her back and chest. There was not quite room for her to draw her knees up double, and she wondered how

Russell could make it, wondered how he had been able to endure his old job, working among men half his size.

Out of nervousness, she wanted to talk as she descended, but it was difficult for him to hear what she was saying; he kept calling "What?" so that she was having to spread her legs and crane her neck and call down to him, as if trying to force the sound waves to sink — like dropping pebbles, she imagined — and in the darkness she could not tell whether he was fifty feet below her or only a few inches. She descended slowly, not wanting to step on his fingers.

Sometimes when she stopped to rest it seemed that the slight curves and tapers of the borehole fit the same curves and tapers of her body, though only in that one resting place; then they would move on, again, descending.

Fantastic paranoias began to plague her as they descended more than one hundred feet. It felt as if they had traveled at least a mile.

The portal of sky above had diminished to less than the size of a penny, and her breath came fast now as she imagined some skulking woodsperson coming upon the telltale scatter of their clothing and finding a boulder to roll over their tomb. She paused and lowered her head to her chest, forced herself to chase the thought from her mind, but there was nowhere for it to go; like a bat, it fled but returned. She felt chilled, and she was seized with the sudden impulse to pee, but held it in.

Fifty feet farther down — moving as slow as a sloth, now — she imagined that they were using up all the air, and another twenty-five feet after that, she imagined that although Russell had been a nice enough young man, a gentleman, on the earth above, the descent and the pressures and swells of the earth would metamorphose him into something awful and raging —

that he might at any second seize her ankle and begin eating her raw flesh, gnawing at her from below.

A trickle of urine escaped. She stopped again, clamped down, hoped that he would not distinguish it from the spring water. Despite the coolness, she was sweating, muddy and gritty now.

There came a grunting sound from below her, piglike in nature, and her heart leapt in terror, certain that the transformation had begun.

"Oh, man," Russell said, "I wish I hadn't eaten so much."

"Are you stuck?"

"No, I've just got to go."

"Can you wait?"

"Yeah."

"How much farther do you think?"

"Any minute. Any time now," he said.

The penny of light above had disappeared completely.

A little later, a little deeper into the hole, she heard Russell cry out in what sounded initially like fear.

"What is it?"

He was right below her, thrashing and bumping, so that at first she thought he was falling.

"What is it?" she asked again. She felt him climbing up below her, his hands and head up around her ankles, and she scooted up quickly, bumping her knees against the wall.

"Oh Christ," he said. "It was a shitload of bones down there. A *wad* of bones. Something must have fallen down the hole and gotten stuck there where it narrows. God," he said, "I was all tangled up in them."

Sissy was quiet for a long while. "What do you think they are?" she said. "Do you think they're human?"

"I guess I should find out," Russell said. He descended

from her ankles back into silence. A few seconds later, she heard the sticklike clattering of bones as he kicked his way through the nest of them: the brittle snapping of ribs and femurs. *God,* she thought, *I will go to church every Sunday for the rest of my life, I will become a nun, I will . . .*

Russell groped around for the different pieces he could reach. "I heard them land," he said. "We're almost to the bottom."

Thank you, Jesus, Sissy thought, not caring now if they were the pope's bones.

"Careful," Russell said, "they'll scratch you some, coming down through them."

"What are they?"

"I don't know," Russell said, and then a moment later, "Okay, I'm on the bottom."

After the constriction of the adit, the space around her was divine: open air all around her, and a set of railroad tracks beneath her feet, tunneling laterally through the coal.

She hunkered down and peed. There was too much space in the total blackness; she felt that if they ventured left or right of the adit, with its lightless surface high above, they would never find it again, but Russell said that they would be able to feel the ladder rungs hammered into the wall and would know also where they were by the tangles of bones beneath it.

"What kind are they?" she asked. She had moved nearer to Russell and reached out to touch his shoulder, and kept her hand there, as would a tired swimmer far out in the ocean who found, strangely, one rock fixed and protruding above the waves. Even that close, she could see nothing of him, though she could feel the heat from the mass of his body.

He crouched and began sifting through the bones, sorting them by feel, nearly all of them long and slender, until he found the skull, which he groped in the darkness: felt the ridges above the eyes, the molars, the eye sockets themselves.

"Deer," he said, and handed her the skull. He could not see where she was, and accidentally pressed the skull into her belly.

She took the skull from him and examined it. The relief that it was not a human seemed to her to give them a freedom, a second chance at something.

"All right," she said, "I guess we can walk a little ways." She reached for, and found, his hand.

"Wait here a second," he said. "I've really got to go."

He left her standing there and walked down the tracks. He was gone a long time. Sissy sat down and wrapped her arms around her knees and waited. She kept her back to the wall. She kept listening for Russell but could hear nothing. She wondered if he had come to some junction in the tracks and had taken a turn and gotten lost.

She had the adit directly above her, or very near her. She could feel the slight upwelling of breeze, still rising as if to a chimney, though she supposed that at nighttime as the air cooled it would begin to sink back down the adit, falling with an accelerated force that might be exhilarating, deafening.

She called out his name but got no answer. He was too shy. It was possible he would walk a mile, maybe farther, before depositing his spoor, to keep from offending her.

If he got lost, all she had to do was stand up, take hold of the rungs in the darkness, and begin climbing back up.

She called his name again. Not only was there no answer, but there was an emptiness that made it seem certain no ears had heard her call. She stood up and began walking in the direction she was certain he had gone.

She walked for a long time. She kept her right hand on the wall at all times, and stretched her left hand out into space, hoping to feel what might lie out there, though there was always nothing.

She came to another adit, and paused; she peered up it, saw no light, and could not be sure whether she felt a breeze or not. She touched the steel spikes, the rungs hammered into the stone, to see if she could discern any human warmth he might have left climbing up them.

She thought that she might be running out of air, and then felt almost certain that she was. A jag of panic shot through her like a spike of lightning — her heart clenched — and she gripped the rungs and started up.

The farther she climbed — five, then ten minutes — the more she began to understand why perhaps she should not have.

There was no water-trickle coming down this shaft; there was no breeze, no dimness of light above.

Her eyes felt as large as eggs. The shaft was tight all around her, too tight, and she longed for the space below. She stopped, dropped her head in momentary defeat, and then descended. The bare stone and grit beneath her bare feet felt good, once she got back down to the bottom. The tunnel was beginning to feel familiar to her. She started walking again, traveling on in the same direction she had been traveling. She came to what she thought was a dead end — a fallen jumble of timbers and stone — but in her groping found a cave-sized opening, a passage — the only one through which he could have passed, if he had indeed come this way — and she squeezed through it.

It was possible that as she climbed, he had passed back by beneath her, searching for her.

She walked deeper, farther into the darkness, wondering what mountain she was passing beneath: wondering what the shape and size of it was, and what birds lived on it; whether there were the houses and homes of humans perched atop it, or if bears lived on it; wondering if cougars hunted deer on its slopes. Wondering if packs of coyotes ran wild through its woods. Wondering if mossy creeks ran down its folds and crevices, and if there were fish in those creeks, and frogs and salamanders.

She walked right into Russell, coming from the other direction; they collided, bumped chests and heads and knees, and caught each other in a tangle of arms and stinging elbows, grabbed each other from reflex, then yelled at each other and leapt away.

"Russell?" she said.

For a moment he considered not answering her, or saying that he was someone else. But the other language — her hands gripping his arm, her knee against his — was already speaking, and they moved into each other, and together, as easily as if the fit were one they had been searching for all along, as if it were not a chance or random stumbling. They sat down, still coupled, and then lay down to love, sprawled yet clinging to each other on the bed of old crushed rubble and ore, blind to the world, blind to everything except the language of touch — so heightened now by the deprivation of other senses that it seemed possible that when they emerged, if they emerged, they might somehow be able to transfer a similar intensity to all of the other senses, and that in so doing, they might stride the earth as strongly and freely as giants. That there was not any one limited reservoir of feeling, but infinite access to the senses, and that after having thus loved, and emerging transformed, metamorphosed, they would see and hear and taste and scent odors with an almost intolerable fullness.

Afterward — still feeling so huge, so alive, as if they could barely fit in the tunnel — they held hands and walked farther, following the tracks.

"Sometimes there are different layers," Russell said. "Adits below adits. We have to be careful not to step into one and fall a hundred feet down to some lower level. In the old days you could be working on one level and feel the mountain shaking when a train of ore passed above or below you."

"How far down do you think this goes?" Sissy asked. "How many layers?"

"It's honeycombed," Russell said, and laughed. "Hell, maybe it goes all the way."

The tunnel veered slightly, or so it seemed — as if it were tracing some contour that might be reflected on the slope of the mountain, out in the green bright outside world. They kept coming to various junctions, taking a left or a right based not on any regular or mappable system of order or logic — two lefts and a right, two lefts and a right — but rather based only on how their hearts felt at each juncture.

A dull scent at one intersection, a bright scent at another. A breath, a bare whisper of a breath, of freshness or dampness. A variance — or so it seemed — in the gravity beneath their naked feet. Anything could make up their mind for them, and they had no earthly idea of their reasoning; they were simply being pulled along by the earth. If they got lost or tired of walking they would stop and make love again.

After some time, they came to one of the abandoned pump-jack boxcars — one of the old manually driven ore carts that used to race up and down the tracks, which a single miner could operate by pumping up and down on a central fulcrum, which rose and fell like a seesaw, with hidden intricate gearings below by which great volumes of mass could be moved — slowly at first, but then with increasing power and speed and efficiency.

They stopped and examined with their hands the shape and coolness of the rust-locked vehicle.

They climbed up on top of it. With his hands, Russell showed Sissy where to sit to stay out of the way of the handle, and by pulling as hard as he could, he was able to slowly make the first downward stroke on the mechanism, breaking it free of years of rust and sleep. The tracks were rusted, as were the steel wheels and axles of the little flatcar itself; but once he got that first downward stroke, the second stroke came easier. The flatcar seemed to lift slightly, and tighten and tense — as did Russell, on the third stroke, down, and the fourth, up.

The boxcar began to inch along, moving no faster than an old man walking crookedly. Slivers and flakes of orange rust, unseen by them, but scented, began to fall from the flatcar.

A slight breeze stirred her hair and cooled her sweat-damp skin. A lone spark tumbled from the front wheels. Sissy could feel the radiant heat from Russell's work — she sat on the other end of the flatcar across from him, so that it was as if she were on the bow of a ship — and slowly, the breeze increased. It swirled her hair in front of her face, and passed cool beneath her arms. She listened to the groaning resistance of the rusty tracks beneath them — a sound like a cat yowling — and wished that she could see him.

More sparks began to spill from the steel wheels, trickling but then pouring from the wheels, so that the lower half of the tunnel, as well as the lower half of each of their bodies, was periodically illuminated as if by orange firelight.

Their passage became easier, faster, and the shower of sparks increased proportionately, her hair swirling all around her and the rooster tail of sparks rising higher around them, revealing in flickering orange light the cave walls; up past their waists, and then past their chests, and then the orange pulses of spark-light rose higher still.

The spray of light rose above their shoulders and finally their faces, so that now all of them was illuminated, as if they had been painted or even created by that light, and by the thunderous noise. As the cave walls raced past, they caught occasional glimpses of old artifacts from the other world: busted out carbon lamps, and pickaxes leaning fifty years against the walls as if the miners had stepped away for only a moment.

They were traveling thirty, forty miles an hour. Sissy leaned forward, peered intently into the onrushing darkness, unable to see beyond the sparks. It was if they were surrounded by a cage of sparks, fire bouncing all around them and leaving glowing ingots in their wake.

Sissy looked back at him — in his feverish, nearly demonic pumping, he seemed to be orange-afire, and as he looked down at her watching him, she seemed calmly likewise — and now the flatcar, the mechanics of its gearings and the momentum of its mass, entered some kind of glide.

The tunnel reverberated and the mountain sang, glowing with traces and movements of life once more — such a roar that it was as if they were gnawing or carving or even blasting their way out of the mountain; and as they hurtled onward, fearless of unseen brick walls or plunge-caverns below, swept by reckless frenzy and daring, Sissy had the slightly troubling feeling (despite her grin, as she leaned out into that black wind) that she was leaving something behind.

Russell was finally beginning to tire. He was slowing down, pumping only three or four times a minute, letting the cart glide and then slowing it to a coast.

A button of light appeared before them. They were confused, not knowing whether the light was above them, or directly ahead of them, or even below: they could no longer be sure now, save for the faint tugging of gravity, which way was up and which down.

As Russell slowed the cart further, the fountain of sparks fell lower, the wall of light fading from their waists and their thighs, until finally the flatcar was drifting so slowly that only their feet were illuminated by occasional bouncing crumbs of orange light.

Russell's body was lathered with sweat; the cart coasted to a complete stop. His heart pounding as wildly as if he had a badger trapped in his chest, he lay down, trembly-legged, on top of Sissy, nestled in to the fit of her, laying his big head on her stomach, and rested. He was so hot that it seemed he might burn her.

They lay there for a long time. Sissy had the thought that he might harden in his cooled position as he slept, like something molten cast from a forge. She licked the dried salt from the hollow of his neck, then licked his chest, to awaken him, fearful that the button of light would disappear, and that they would not be able to find it again.

He sat up, stiff, and spit out a little blood, which he could taste but not see. He coughed again — splashed another spray of it across the walls, unseen — the silicosis, the lung-lattice of scars, clenching within him as his body realized where he was once again, as if in an allergic reaction.

They rested a while longer and then climbed down from the

flatcar and began walking toward the light, once more holding hands. It was all she could do to keep from dropping his hand and racing toward that light.

The wind coming from behind them grew stronger closer to the cave's exit. Sissy leaned forward — the dull light bright enough now for them to see vaguely the pale dull outlines of each other's bodies — the ball of light was the size of a melon, and so close; again, she wanted to drop his hand and run — but Russell wanted to make love again, there at the edge of light, and so with a strange reluctance she let him pull her down to where he was sitting on the tracks, on the bed of ore. She was too sore to take him so he worked between her legs, and around the shape of her; as he kissed her, she could taste the blood, could scent the odor of it coming from his lungs, and when he had finished, his concluding tremors lured his lungs into another paroxysm of blood-spray, so that he was barely able to pull away in time, and heaved the mist of blood-spray across her back rather than into her mouth.

They lay in silence a short while — he apologized; she said nothing, only squeezed his hand.

They got up and walked on toward the light, the blood sticky across both of them. Sissy could taste the clean air. It seemed that a rain shower had passed during the time they had been beneath the mountain — there was that smell in the air, as well as the scent of flowers and wild strawberries — and the sunlight looked washed, scrubbed.

The opening was now its full size, its full self. The light was fully upon them. Sissy was afraid Russell would want to pull her down yet again, but instead he followed her out into the sunlight where the tracks ended. They turned around and looked up at the forested mountain above them, having no idea where they were. Sissy felt like weeping, so strange and beautiful was the sight of the real world.

They studied each other for the first time in the full light of late afternoon: blood and semen splattered, red grit and coal-dust caked, wild haired, but beautiful to each other.

They bathed by wading through the brush, which was still wet from the afternoon's shower. They scrubbed themselves with leafy green branches, then began walking carefully on bare feet through the woods, contouring around the mountain, hoping to somehow stumble across the piles of their clothes.

The sunlight seemed different — as if they had been gone for months, so that now they had emerged into a different season; or that perhaps they had been gone for centuries, even millennia, so that the tilt and angle of things was slightly different — the sunlight casting itself against the earth in some ancient or perhaps newer pattern.

They moved through the bronze light carefully, searching for where they had been. They could hear no roads below. They passed beneath sun-dappled canopy, through beams and columns of gold-green light where the sun poured down through sweetgum, beech, oak, and hickory. They could taste the green light on their bodies. It was a denser, more humid light — almost as if they were moving around underwater. Sissy saw that Russell was becoming aroused yet again — that he was like some kind of monster, in this regard — and she hurried into a trot, only half-playing, to stay ahead of him.

Later in the afternoon, they found a patch of wild strawberries and crawled through them on their hands and knees, sometimes plucking the tiny wild berries but other times bending down and grazing them straight from the plants.

They kept contouring around the mountain. They surprised a doe and fawn, who jumped up from their day bed and stood staring at them for the longest time before finally flagging their tails and cantering off into the woods.

The pieces of the puzzle began to come together slowly. They heard the faint sound of a road. They found a skein of rock, an outcropping, similar to one they had seen earlier in the day. They followed the strike of it a little farther up the mountain, believing themselves to be too low. The sound of the highway grew closer, disturbingly monotonous and familiar, yet they moved toward it, knowing their clothes to be somewhere in that vicinity, and when they finally found them, having come full circle around the little mountain, they sat down on a boulder in the last angle of light and stared for a while at their crumpled and folded clothes, not wanting to climb back into them, and they studied the cleft, the passage, beneath which so much had happened.

They marveled at the notion that if, or when, they walked away from it, the memory of it would be held bright and strong within them for a long time, but that after a longer time — after they were gone — the memory would begin to fade and lithify until it was all but forgotten, invisible: that even an afternoon such as that one could become dust.

They dressed only because they had to and walked slowly down toward the sound of the road. Soon they could catch the glimpses of cars, colored flecks of metal, racing past on the road below, caught in glimpses between the limbs and leaves of the trees. Their own car, with the green canoe atop, waiting as if resting, ready to rejoin the unaltered flow of things. Descending, again.

Presidents' Day

JERRY AND KAREN WERE two weeks shy of their seventeenth wedding anniversary when an acquaintance of Jerry's, Jim, called to say that he had fallen down while splitting wood and detached a retina, losing sight in one eye. He had driven himself to the emergency clinic, where he had been referred to an eye specialist in Spokane, four hours away. Jim had been an officer in the navy but was retired now; he was forty-eight. He was old-school, unaccustomed to and uncomfortable asking for anyone else's help. On his drive to Spokane, the retina had occasionally shifted back into a rough approximation of its proper position and, for a few seconds, Jim would again be able to see out of that injured eye, a vague haze of gray-white light, before everything went black again.

In Spokane, the examining surgeon, a twenty-year navy man himself, Dr. Le Page, had canceled the ski trip he'd planned with his teenage son to perform the emergency reattachment surgery. Unable to find a nurse on such short notice — it was Presidents' Day — he'd had his son fill in, still attired in his bright skiwear, complete with bob-tasseled jester's hat.

That had been four days ago, and Jim was supposed to lie on his back several hours of each day, perfectly still, while the retina, that thin filter between the brain and the outside world, tried to reattach itself to the back of the eyeball. Because Dr. Le

Page forbade Jim to drive, Jim was calling to see if Jerry might be able to run him back over to Spokane for his first checkup to see if the retina had fully attached. Dr. Le Page had told Jim that there was a 95 percent chance that everything would be all right and they'd be able to turn around and head right back home.

Jerry was surprised, and slightly flattered, that Jim had asked him for help. He told Jim he'd check with Karen but, although he didn't tell Jim, he suspected Karen would fall out of her seat in her eagerness to get him out of the house.

If their story was not the most ancient in the world, it had to be running a close second: the end of love. The flat water where the shore is no longer visible, and where all wind leaves the sails, and the sun hangs overhead for days, without moving, in a bright burning haze, a searing ball of light, nothing more. A place where both will and navigation fail, as does the imagination, and where the two sailors, the two castaways, finally have no choice — none — but to turn upon each other: a place where each has finally become the other's prisoner.

One sailor — suppose he is a man much like Jerry — rides in the bow, and in the doldrums' heat feels as if he is burning at the stake. He turns in the seat of the little boat and tries to speak to the other sailor — she might be a woman much like Karen — but it is as if no sound comes from his mouth, or if it does, as if the words fall into some chasm before they ever reach her, across even that short distance.

Suppose that a hundred, or ten thousand lashes, however faint or light each one might be on its own, have mounted across the years: ten thousand little lashes or harshnesses or tak-ing-for-granted ignorings, for every one small and dwindling kindness. Will you fold the newspaper more neatly when you're done with it, can't you do anything right? Why must you lift the lid of a pot on the stove to see what's cooking when it should be evident to anyone with any intelligence by the damned odor alone that I'm cooking rice, and that it's sitting there steaming, as it needs to do, and that now you've let all the steam out? And, *goddammit,* you bought the wrong kind of milk at the grocery store, *I told you to get the one percent with the blue label at the top, not the fucking one and a half percent with the red label! Don't you pay attention to anything, can't you observe what's in the refrigerator each day?*

Panicked, the one sailor stares at his attacker, his critic. *We're stranded on open water,* he wants to whisper, *we've got to pull together* — but mid-sea, she can no longer hear or even see him, and instead stares right through and past him. The man — yes, certainly, it is Jerry, and perhaps he is not the only one — continues to feel that he is burning at the stake; he is filled with despair that she is wasting the moment, wasting the last moments.

They float.

Occasionally the sailor in the stern shifts her focus, notices that the passenger in front is speaking to her, or is trying to speak to her. She can't be sure, but the expression on her face makes it appear that he is asking something of her — that he wants something from her, something she doesn't have anymore — and even though she can no longer hear him, she can see that he keeps asking, and it makes her hate him. There's nowhere to put the hate, however, on such a wide, flat sea, and so she just holds on to it, and the boat grows more leaden.

He tries to be more perfect, or less imperfect. Despite the fading tenure of their years together, he buys her flowers each day that he is in town. In cold weather, if she is to go out somewhere in her car, he makes a point of warming the vehicle up for her and backing it sufficiently far out of the garage so that the fumes from the idling engine do not build up in the garage, but not so far that she has to walk out into the snow. But one morning, when she's running late, it turns out that he has positioned the car so that its door brushes against the garage wall when opened, thereby limiting somewhat the space available for her to slip in behind the driver's seat; and because she has an armload, that morning — a purse, a shoulder bag, and a cup of coffee — she exhales her familiar sound of exasperation, shakes her head, and mutters, once again, *How hard would it be, really, to do something right the first time?*

She's a beautiful woman, even now into her mid-forties — in some respects more beautiful than ever, and it's true that people have always all but fallen over themselves doing for her — often she needs not even to make a request, but simply look or suggest or, sometimes, point, in order to urge the doer along. But Jerry, more than anyone, knows she has also a beautiful heart, that it, that great heart, resides like a mask behind a mask beneath a mask, and that only he can see far enough back there — past the false or surface beauty, and then behind the false or surface anger, buried just behind that skin's beauty, all the way to the contemplative tenderness he knows is still alive far within her.

Jerry is a stonemason — a creative enough occupation but one in which, always, limitations and stress loads are understood — the rock, or span of bricks, able to do only certain things, in the end, and able to achieve only certain effects and certain goals, within reason. There are no miracles in his job, only the daily cumulative force of showing up each day and putting in one's careful and cautious hours as precisely and diligently as possible, with the shape of the work manifesting itself not in any one hour's or one day's labors but over the course of the project's entirety.

And it's not always out-and-out war; there's reason for hope. Karen's an artist, and possesses an artist's volition, sure, but just as frequent as the pustulous outbursts of frenzied rage and fear (he thinks) at the proximity of his ponderous, outsized heart are the long stretches of silence and invisibility; as if neither time nor matter exists, as if the days and nights are not rushing past, being funneled down a drain; as if there is no urgency; and as if Karen believes Jerry is content to receive, forever, those faint lashings and faint withholdings.

Still, the calm water, horrible as it is, never lasts.

Occasionally they stir, and fight like crows or magpies, squabbling over the last of that water, Jerry believing she still has some left in the vessel which she is not sharing and Karen knowing that she does not.

"You make me *puke*," the one sailor cries to the other one on some of the days when her numbness fades and she returns to war. "You *repulse* me."

And always, he retreats and sits on the other end of the boat, bow or stern, and watches the horizon, as he has for so many years now, still hoping for a shore, and still — amazingly — believing that there is another shore out there.

When Jerry asked her if she minded if he drove Jim back over to Spokane, at first Karen didn't understand what Jerry was saying. She had to ask him to repeat himself twice more and couldn't figure out what Jim had to do with it: why someone whom Jerry didn't know that well would have to request help from another person who, if not a stranger, was neither a committed friend. She didn't understand the depth of the need, the seriousness of Jim's situation.

She watched Jerry slip out of the boat and into the warm

sheen of flat water. Something caught her attention at the corner of her vision — she frowned, squinted, turned her head to look at it — and when she returned her gaze to the ocean before her, the calm sea, he was gone, leaving not even a ripple.

When Jerry picked Jim up at his cabin before first light, it was foggy and the roads were covered with a glaze of ice that glinted in their headlights. They had to drive slowly, and in the last wedge of darkness before dawn, deer tiptoed back and forth across the road in front of them, returning to the daytime sanctuary of the woods after having ventured earlier in the night down to the river's frozen edge for a drink of water from the current's fast-flowing center. The deer trotted back across the glassine road on tiny black hoofs, slipping occasionally, their eyes glowing red in the headlights.

The retina is the last screen through which any incoming light passes, before flooding into the brain, where the light proceeds to tell its stories and be processed, stored, and filed as memory and knowledge; because the eyes are so important to a sense of orientation, any disruptions to them can send the body into a state of extreme confusion. Not knowing why, the body often responds with an agonizing form of nausea, not unlike the throes of seasickness, trying to purge anything and everything it might have taken in, on the off chance that that's what's causing the problem.

Jim was seized by this nausea from time to time and would ask Jerry to pull over to the side of the road so that he could retch. Sometimes Jim would have nothing left in his stomach to hurl, and would succeed in vomiting only a thin trickle of shining drool; other times he would be able to make it a short distance into the woods, stumbling down the twists and turns of frozen deer trails, before expelling, in coughs and gags, the detritus of his stomach.

Jim's face was still swollen and bruised from the previous surgery — the injured eye, the left one, was still almost completely shut — and he wasn't much company, though he tried to be stoic about it, riding upright with his head held in his hands, swaying with the road's rough passages, and making random conversation in the lulls between pain and nausea.

He told Jerry that he'd had all sorts of medical repairs done to him just before he got out of the service, to take advantage of the full health care offered by the navy. He'd had knee surgery to pick out all the little fragments of cartilage that had been floating around behind his kneecaps, and had had both ACLs tightened and tuned while the surgeons were working in there. He'd had six crowns put in by the dentist — Jim's teeth flashed and gleamed like a minefield when he smiled, so much gold and silver that it seemed his mouth, and his smile, would be heavy from carrying so much weight. He had a tendon reconstructed in his elbow, too, and a bulging disk removed from his backbone, and had never felt so good. He'd had radical orthokeratology performed so that his vision had been twenty-twenty, and the doctor had noticed the beginning of cataracts, so he'd repaired that problem, too, implanting translucent plastic disks in the place where the cataracts had once been. The cosmetic effects of this surgery were strangely troubling to Jerry, for sometimes when the light hit Jim's eyes at just the right angle it reflected off those plastic disks set behind the cornea, causing Jim's eyes to shine not unlike those of the deer that passed before their headlights.

"In many respects, I'm like an entirely new man," Jim said. He laughed. "Older and better. Who would've believed it? Except for this darned eye."

Jim had grown up in the sand hills of Nebraska, dreaming of the ocean. "I'd always been restless and daring," he told Jerry. "When I was in high school my friend and I stole a plane from the county airport, even though we didn't know how to fly, and we crashed it. That's how I first hurt my back. I went back the next year, got my pilot's license, rented one legal, but then crashed it, too — flew it through a power line." He lifted his arm to show Jerry the scars. "Had to have a steel plate put in my arm. It sets off the metal detector in airports." He tapped his teeth. "Sometimes my teeth pick up radio waves, too. Late at night, driving in flat country, I can pick up those big high-powered Christian stations." He laughed. "Talk about hearing voices in your head! Drives me fucking crazy, sometimes. Driving out toward Nebraska once, going back to visit family, I couldn't make the broadcast stop, so I had to turn around and drive back up into the mountains, and wait there for daylight, for the station to go off the air. It's funny sometimes how much you take peace and quiet for granted: how nothing can be sweeter than just a little space and time where you're not hurting or in anguish about anything."

Jerry nodded. In the last couple of years he had taken to going out by himself to a little cabin he'd built away from the main house and reading by candlelight for an hour or two, and drinking a glass of wine or two, sometimes big glasses — sometimes three glasses — before coming back in to go to bed, where sometimes Karen would still be sitting up, propped against a pillow, reading and drinking, though other times already asleep, and the inside of the house as silent as if it were already abandoned: as if they had already lived the full reach of their lives and passed on into dust and then history and then nothingness. Jerry had grown up on the Texas Gulf coast, within reach of full sight and scent of the ocean, and had wanted to move away from it, to higher ground, all his life; often, as a child, he'd had dreams of rising tides and floodwaters.

"I guess I'm the exact opposite," he said. "A steady trudger, that's what I am."

"I know that about you," said Jim, smiling and reaching over and clapping a hand on Jerry's shoulder. "That's why I called." He smiled again, as if to say, *There are no secrets in the world, no masks above masks, no masks below masks,* and asked, "How's Karen?"

They kept stopping to eat. Jerry wasn't hungry, but Jim, in his nervousness about finding out whether the first surgery had been successful, was ravenous. They stopped first at a Burger King, and then a McDonald's, and then, most disastrously, a Taco Bell; after each meal, Jim would have to stop a few miles down the road and spit up again, as his body rebelled against these repeated attempts at gaining nourishment, and Jerry said nothing but wondered why in the hell Jim kept going back and doing the same thing, again and again, trapped so distressingly between nausea and hunger.

They arrived early, but Dr. Le Page was already in and waiting for Jim. After a brief examination, he told him that the news was not good: the first surgery had not been successful, and a second, alternative surgery would be required. They would have to stay overnight.

The retina is designed to cling to the back of the eyeball like the thinnest piece of Saran Wrap, fastened to the eye with nothing more than a few cells' width of adhesion. A poet looking at a retina held in her gloved hand during an operation described it as "a strong and durable and beautiful outpost of the brain, as it awaits to be reattached to a gorgeous wall that looks like the inside of an abalone shell, with all its shimmering, radiant iridescence."

Jim's doctor explained it less poetically, comparing it to a sheet of wallpaper that he hoped to hang back in place upon the curved back of the eyeball, hoping that it would not slide off or pull loose again, that it would rest in its proper place long enough for the living cells to grow back between the thin wrap of the retina and the blood-slicked arc of the inner eye.

In the first operation he had sewn a tiny buckle into the back of Jim's eye and had then laced the retina to that buckle. He'd shown Jim the buckle before sewing it on; it had been about the size of a small stainless steel staple. The nylon thread used for the sewing was about the diameter of a single long strand of a woman's hair.

This type of operation was successful about 95 percent of the time, and its surprising failure had caused Jim to consider for the first time that which he had previously been purposefully avoiding — the realization that he might never get back his sight in that eye.

The second, alternative operation — called the bubble procedure — was successful only about 75 percent of the time; if it failed and a third treatment was needed, and then a fourth or a fifth, the percentages continued to decline dramatically.

After Jim got the bad news, they sat for a long time in the waiting room. Jim apologized to Jerry for the two of them having now to stay overnight.

"Hell, don't worry about that," Jerry said. "I'm just sorry you didn't get the answer you wanted. I hate that they have to go in there and work on it again."

"After this operation, I have to keep my head pointed down at the ground for a week," Jim said. The retina had only partially attached the last time, so Dr. Le Page would have to go back in there and cut it loose and burn away all the old scar tissue with lasers, then hang the weary retina back in its proper place. At that point, the doctor would pump a bubble of nitrogen gas right behind the retina, packing the eye socket tight to prevent the retina from slipping loose again, until the connective tissues of life could reclaim it, reattaching and binding it to the back of the eye. That was the reason that Jim would have to keep his head tipped down for several days — to keep the bubble, tucked back in there like a Ping-Pong ball, from sliding to one side or another, wherein the retina, the wallpaper, might slide off.

Near-perfect calm and stillness would be required for the next six to seven days, to keep the bubble balancing there, like an egg perched not even in the cup of a spoon, but on the inverted arc of the spoon overturned — inflated tight-but-not-too-tight against the precarious curve of his eye.

Jim slumped in the outpatient chair. It was a beautiful day outside, nothing but blue sky with bright late-winter sunshine. "I don't even mind the six or seven days," Jim said. "I just mind the not-knowing for that period of time. I'll do anything to get my sight back. Anything. Whatever it takes," he said, "sign me up for it. Anything."

The second operation was scheduled for later in the afternoon; they had six or seven more hours to kill, though Jim showed no inclination toward doing anything but remaining slumped in that chair.

"I thought it was all right," he said. "I thought that because I could see patches of light, it was going to be okay." He sighed deeply. "I knew I was fucked though when he held up two fingers and I couldn't see them. He held them right in front of my face, and still I couldn't see them. Just black."

He slumped farther into his seat.

"The nurses all kept saying how lucky I was to have him — that he's the best in the Northwest," Jim said. "They said he's a miracle worker." Jim shrugged, talking more to himself than to Jerry. "I don't know. I will say this, he's a joker; he did try to make me feel better. It was kind of weird, and only a little bit funny, but at least he was trying.

"After he'd told me the bad news, he left me alone there for a minute to digest it. Said he had to go look at an x-ray. What he really did though was put on this disguise, one that made him look a little different. It was pretty real-looking, especially since I could see just out of the one eye. He was wearing a wig that was just slightly different from how his real hair was, and he had this fake rubber nose, again very realistic, that was just a little different from his real one — longer, and more angular. He had on a slightly different set of eyeglasses, too — not wildly different from the ones he'd been wearing, but a little different, so that you'd notice something had changed — and he was wearing a different smock, one that said 'Doctor Smock' instead of 'Doctor Le Page.'

"When he saw me give him a double take, he laughed and said, 'I'm not Doctor Le Page, I'm Doctor Smock. Don't worry, you're not going crazy: it happens all the time. Everyone thinks there's just one of us — or sometimes they think we're twins!' He folded his clipboard to his chest and sidled in closer, far cheerier than Doctor Le Page had been. 'What's that old buzzard been telling you — that the odds are long you'll ever see again?' He leaned in close to my eye, spread it open with his fingers a little, and clucked. 'I don't know what that old buzzard told you —'

"'He didn't tell me anything,' I said.

"'But I can tell you're going to be okay. Everything's going to be all right. He's a piece of shit, socially, that Doctor Le Page, but it's true what they say, he's a fine surgeon, and I can tell it's going to turn out all right.' Then he left the room," Jim said, "and a minute later, he came back in, himself once more — Dr. Le Page — pretending not to know what was going on.

"It was too weird," Jim said. "Man, I'll tell you what, I am fucking wiped out. Can you imagine?" he said, his anger starting to rise. "What the fuck do you think he was thinking? It was just too weird. He must have gone to a shitload of time and trouble to get it all made up, manufactured just right, so that it seemed only a little different rather than a lot different." He shook his head. "It was so weird. There wasn't much change in him. Just one or two little things. He was hardly any different at all."

The nurse, who had been listening as she filled out some forms at the typewriter, gave them a look that said clearly she'd heard enough moping, that it was time to move out and forward — to clear a space for the next patient. Through his one good eye, and sunk in his pensiveness, Jim noticed none of this, but Jerry said, "Come on, it's a fine day. Let's go outside," and got him up and moving, and they made their way outside, back to their truck.

Jim had made reservations for them to stay at the navy base, and they stopped for lunch at a barbecue place on the way out to it. Several enlisted men came and went, young and hale in their camouflage fatigues, crewcuts, and heavy shining boots.

They drove on to the base. Jim cautioned Jerry to slow down. There were twenty-mile-per-hour speed limit signs posted around the schools, the commissary, the churches, and the hospital — and these limits were enforced totally, zealously, so that all the traffic slowed to a creep in these areas, and coming in from the wild bustle of the outside world, Jerry was disoriented by the effect. It was as if they had wandered or even descended into someplace where time, if not suspended from its usual rapid and alarming rate of decomposition, was at least slowed or postponed.

They registered at the lobby of the guest housing compound — a long row of brick apartments that reminded Jerry of the kind that college students live in, or newly married couples following their first years out of college. There was a kitchen, a tiny bedroom, and a main room with a hide-a-bed, and Jim reeled into the bedroom, exhausted, and collapsed as if into a coma.

Jerry sat down on the couch and tried to read but was made antsy by the grim cinder-block interior of the place, and he watched the cold sunlight through the window gratefully, drinking it in but too weary to get up and go out into it. During each of the seventeen years that Jerry had lived with Karen up in the mountains, the winters had gotten harder and harder for him, psychologically, and though he had not been bothered by it when he was younger, Jerry had come to believe in what the physicians were now calling "seasonal affective disorder," where a person in a gray climate becomes sadder during the light-stricken, shortened days of winter. His fatigue wasn't that simple, he knew, but was present on top of any other weariness, and it seemed to him that the debilitating effect of the winter-sadness was cumulative, like that of too many concussions, the true harm of which is sometimes not revealed until years after the initial injury.

Some years, enduring the winter-sadness was like taking a beating, and the flat-water place of their marriage made the beating worse. Karen went days without touching him, and there were days when she did not seem to like it when he touched her. Sometimes, however, right before falling asleep, they would hold hands, in that last half-minute of wakefulness. Had Jerry become a less interesting person over the years? He didn't think so, but was it possible that a lifetime of stacking rocks, one after the other, had conspired to make her believe that he had? That she had heard and seen all that he had, finally, to offer?

Jerry knew that he wouldn't be able to be a stonemason forever: already he found he was having to use smaller and smaller rocks, using the larger ones only as capstones to save his strength and energy; and some day, all the wear and tear — cartilage and ligament damage, back failure, arthritis, and finally, general and overwhelming old-man's weakness — would deprive him of the solace he found in his work, and that saddened him, though he tried not to think about it overmuch.

He disliked the winter more and more each year, resenting the way it covered up all the stones in the quarry so that he had to wait until spring to select the rocks he would be using in his coming year's work, and he disliked, too, the way the snow covered not just those loose fieldstones on projects unfinished from the autumn before but also all his completed projects. He missed most of all the feeling he got at the end of each day's work, at dusk, when he would look back with pride at the advance of his work, matching comfortably the advance of the summer day, and of how he would always, then, begin to think of Karen with deep hope and deep love, always with hope and love, and would leave his unfinished rock wall, always unfinished, and head on back home, truly eager for another try, no matter how the day had started out upon leaving home that morning.

In the old days, when Karen had to leave a note for him, she would always sign it, "Love, K," even if they had had a squabble earlier that day. But now if there has been even the slightest problem, much less an eruption — suppose Jerry has put a stamp on an envelope crookedly, giving rise to the risk, in Karen's opinion, of the letter's recipient getting the impression that Jerry is a "hayseed," then Karen will omit the "Love, K" part and will leave the note, the instructions, unsigned — as if it, love, or the mention or reaffirmation of it, is a reward to be dispensed or taken away dependent upon execution of behavior, or even upon the sheer horoscopical luck, or unluck, of the day. As if it is a commodity, a finite resource prone to being earned and bartered or lost, rather than something that moves in wild currents of breath writhing in gibbous ribbons across the sky.

There at Jim's old navy base, Jerry sat remembering once again the hope he used to feel at the end of each day's work, and he watched the bright yellow winter sunlight for a long time before emerging from his saddened paralysis and hauling himself out into the sunlight, where he stood in the cold for a long time, ankle deep in snow in the front yard, with his face turned upward, his arms spread wide and lifted loosely to the sky, eyes shut, and felt dully the sun's touch upon his bare face, and the faint warmth of it through his eyelids.

He stood like that for a long time, until his arms grew heavy, and even after he had lowered them he remained standing there, head tipped down and shoulders rounded, like an old horse in a barnyard, or an old hound.

When Jim awoke, there was little more than an hour left before the second surgery. He was groggy and silent, and though he did not seem to Jerry to be entirely accepting of his fate, whatever that might be, there was a new resolve about him, as if the despair and confusion, though not banished, had been put aside for however long it would take to get through the operation.

In some ways, this brittle steadiness by Jim was harder for Jerry to be around than Jim's previous worries. It seemed to Jerry now that there was the feeling that a bomb was about to go off, that terror and blackness was but a thin scratch beneath the surface.

Jim knew he'd be wiped out after the surgery and wanted to go by the commissary beforehand, both to stock up on items for his trip home and to get something nice for Jerry's dinner that night, still concerned that Jerry would have to be spending the night away from home.

"Karen won't mind, will she?" he asked again.

"No," Jerry said, "she won't mind."

"I'm sorry I won't be much company this evening," he said. They were each carrying a basket. Jim knew he'd want a beer afterward, and maybe some ice cream and yogurt.

"It's okay," Jerry said.

The commissary was an explosion of bounty and light. The high overhead fluorescent lights glared and reflected in all directions, and the floor was sparkling white. The plastic wrappings of each product glinted under the high pulsing lights, and the aisles of the store were crowded with shoppers pushing steel carts piled to overflowing with packages — toilet paper, of course, and five-liter bottles of Diet Coke, and sponges, and potato chips. The commissary was as crowded with retired military personnel as it was with those still serving in active duty, and it was the retired soldiers and sailors who seemed most determined, willful, to exploit the benefits of their previous enlistment, though in their movements they bore also a vacationlike camaraderie. Jerry watched with fascination as the ex-soldiers, men and women, middle-aged and old-aged, pushed those shopping carts up and down the aisles like looters.

Frozen pizzas for a dollar, cans of soda pop a dime each. Plastic binoculars for their grandchildren, cartoon videos for two dollars. Jelly beans, coffee beans, and fifty-pound sacks of navy beans. The prices all seemed arrested, as if halted in their natural growth twenty-five or thirty years ago, or even longer; and the old sailors and infantrymen, the battleship mechanics and howitzer specialists, the Seals and the Green Berets, fell upon these prices, these offerings, voracious now in their waning years to get back some fragment of all that which they had given. As if it might all yet balance.

After a while the intensity of the shopping made Jerry a little queasy, and he was reminded, in almost hallucinogenic fashion, of a vast warehouse filled with tens of thousands of termites or carpenter ants, each one chewing and gnawing in full frenzy, eating out the hollowed middle of a structure that was sure to collapse at any moment, and he could barely stand to stay inside any longer.

After Jim paid for his purchases and came back outside, Jim tilted his head to look up at the winter sky. A thin sheet of haze was advancing upon the sun, a shoal of clouds bringing in weather from the west. Jim glanced at his watch. He had thirty minutes left before his operation, and Jerry felt that he too was under the gun — that though he might have slightly more time than Jim, the clock was beginning to move fast for him too, now, and that he himself might have only two or three days left before some final or important convocation, summons, or termination — though what powerful event might rest in his own destiny, and such a short notice away, he could not begin to say.

By the time they got to the clinic, Jim was more jittery than ever, and it did not help matters that everyone else in the crowded waiting room appeared to be as old as Methuselah. Except for the nurses, interns, and physicians, Jim and Jerry were the only citizens of vigor present.

The clinic was set up to maximize a steady high-volume flow of clients, with all the surgeons working on all the patients in a great common room, just beyond the receptionist's desk. The operating room was separated from the waiting area by only a glass wall, so that the friends and family could stand and watch the progress of the operation. They couldn't necessarily see the details, but they could see the doctor-in-blue bent over the skull of their patient and could tell by the patient's stillness the depth of the anesthesia's hold or, by the groggy stirrings, the degree of recovery. The operating room was lit brilliantly and had about it the air of a large and busy garage on a Friday evening, with all the mechanics hurrying to finish in time for the weekend.

Most of the mates and accomplices of the patients chose however to ignore the glass wall and sat with their heads tucked in magazines, or fretting with needlework or cross-stitch, chatting with one another about, among other things, the number of times they had been to Branson, Missouri. Jerry listened to one such conversation that went on for ten minutes about a split pea soup that had evidently been a staple of a cafeteria there, as well as a favorite of both seniors. Then they began talking about the prune pies they had had for dessert.

Jerry got up and stood at the wall for a long time and tried to watch his friend, but Jim was wheeled to the very back of the room and Dr. Le Page had his own back turned to the wall, so that all Jerry could see were Jim's big feet. After a while he sat back down and read a book, surrounded by the casual, almost dreamy murmurings of the sighted.

Jim and Jerry had been told the surgery would take only one hour, but it was three and a half hours before Jim emerged, his face even more swollen and discolored, with a pirate's eye patch and mummy-wrap swathing the entire left side. Dr. Le Page did not seem to be up to any of his tricks that time, and he went out of his way to meet with Jerry and to tell him that he felt confident that he had gotten it right this time, and Jerry could see, for the first time, in both Dr. Le Page's confidence and terseness, how much the doctor had been bothered by the failure of the first surgery.

"It took a long time because we had to burn off a lot of scar tissue," Dr. Le Page said, using that curious vernacular "we" that so many professionals employ, even when they are the only one involved in an act. "We also inflated the bubble behind the retina extra large, to be sure the retina doesn't slip. For a few days the eye might be a little more painful than it would have been otherwise, but I think it's worth it. I wanted to be absolutely sure this time."

Jim was still groggy from the anesthesia, so Dr. Le Page made sure that Jerry understood what he was saying — handed him the prescription for pain medicines, which he said Jim would definitely be needing. "The bubble will dissolve slowly," Dr. Le Page explained, "with the gas being absorbed first into the bloodstream, and then expelled back into the outer atmosphere via the lungs. As the bubble slowly dissipates, his vision will return. Right now he won't be able to see around the bubble — it'll be like trying to see around a brick wall — but in time, as the bubble subsides, light will be able to reenter the brain. It was a good surgery," Dr. Le Page said, with confidence. "He'll be able to see again.

"He's going to have about a two-hour grace period," Dr. Le Page said, "before the anesthesia wears off and he starts feeling really, really sick." Jerry nodded and shook hands with Dr. Le Page, who had already stepped out of his blue scrub suit; beneath it he was wearing a dapper gray houndstooth suit with a bright blue tie, and a starched white shirt, and black dress shoes. After having spent the previous day clinging to the belief that $5,000 an hour was usurious, Jerry found himself of the opinion now that it was a bargain; or that any price, high or low, was irrelevant, compared to the worth and beauty and wonder of Jim's full eyesight being returned to him.

Jim had to walk with his head pointed straight down at the ground so that he could see, through his one good but fatigued eye, no farther than the tips of his shoes, and Jerry took Jim by the crook of the arm.

Even in his drugged stupor, Jim resented the help, or the fact that he needed the help, and sought to pull free from Jerry's supporting hand, but after he did so he found himself standing alone in the parking lot, still staring down at his shoes, without a clue as to where their truck was parked; and so he had to relent and submit to being led and guided, helped — though it would only, he told himself, be for seven days. Soon enough, he would be fierce and strong and independent again, and this period of need, of deep need, would pass like a breeze, like a summer day, like a scrap of bright, colorful cloth blown by the wind.

It was as Dr. Le Page had predicted; they had not been back at their room for more than an hour (foolishly, stubbornly, Jim had drunk a quart of beer and eaten a pint of ice cream) before the anesthesia faded and the agony struck.

It began as the low, vague awareness of pain deep in the center of his skull, like a dull fire that soon enough catches a breath of oxygen and burns brightly; and this escalating pain (his eye soon felt as if a horse had stepped on it) was coupled quickly with an explosion of nausea and diarrhea.

It was the worst of both worlds: the pain made Jim want nothing more than to curl up on the bed, hunched on his hands and knees, motionless, in order to keep the bubble in his head tipped perfectly level — and yet the roils of nausea demanded that he stagger from the bed every five minutes and make his way into the bathroom to expel the toxins and confusions of his illness.

Dr. Le Page had prescribed pills for both the nausea and the pain, and Jim began to take them in earnest — first one, then a second, and a third, and a fourth — but either they weren't powerful enough for the magnitude of his torment or he was simply jetting them back out with his diarrhea before they could be absorbed into his bloodstream, for his agony continued unabated.

Jerry felt terrible that there was nothing he could do. He got up and went out to fetch a bag of ice for Jim to place over the injured eye, but it was no use, nothing was of any use, and Jerry finally had to place his head under the pillows of the hide-a-bed to try to drown out the sound of Jim's thrashings and convulsions in the next room.

All night long Jim shifted and groaned, trying unsuccessfully to find some middle place of numbness between nausea and agony; and there was no part in him, not one cell of either hope or memory, that could see or imagine an end to the misery.

The gas bubble he sought to balance so perfectly at the back of his eye was suppressing the function of the tear duct, so that even as he imagined that his injured eye was tearing, watering profusely, no fluids were emerging from that eye — there was only a dry and rapid anguished blinking and twitching — nor were any tears produced in the eye's sympathetic partner, the uninjured one.

Jerry slept fitfully as well, his slumber interrupted by Jim's ceaseless comings and goings, and even lonely as he was, chained to a gray-sky marriage, Jerry recognized the degree and value of his freedom: the absence of physical pain or even ailment. The love in his marriage was not the amount he had once had, when they'd first been in love and he had been unable to do any wrong in the eyes of his beloved, or even later, when she had still loved him fiercely even as his myriad imperfections and flaws and failings were revealed; but he was still strong and healthy, and there was still the hope of tomorrow: always, so much hope.

A thousand times, ten thousand times, he'd pleaded with Karen to let go of her disappointment with his multitudinous flaws and her decision (he was convinced it was a conscious choice) to remain bored. He had pleaded with her to pick up the oars and begin rowing — to strike for the far shore, even though it was unseen — even as he was slowly beginning to understand more fully each day that the issue was out of his hands.

A wind would pick up out over the water and catch the sail, or it would not. She had thrown her oars away, and when in the spirit of hope and conciliation he had handed her his, she had thrown them away, too.

Did she think she was going to live to be a hundred?

Did she think there was going to be another chance? *Wake up,* he wanted to tell her.

Memory, scudding in beneath him:

In their mid-thirties, they had gone up to northern Michigan to visit the Great Lakes. They had gone late in the year, to avoid all the tourists, and had rented a cabin far back in the woods, on the frozen western shore of Lake Superior. The golden leaves of birch trees had already been stripped, as had the oranging needles of the tamarack, though no snow had fallen yet. They had stayed there three days, with a fire burning constantly in the wood stove, and had dressed warmly and gone for walks along the beach, wandering slowly and stopping often to examine the wave-polished stones, collecting the prettier ones in burlap sacks to take back home.

Their next-to-last night, a storm blew in from the north, tearing not just the last of the leaves from the trees but entire limbs and branches, so that in the morning, when they went for their walk, they had to step carefully over an incredible latticework of fallen branches, with the scent of freshly crushed boughs' thick sap sweet upon the colder air. Then, farther on, once they were out on the open beach and past the wreckage of the trees, they began to encounter a curious clustering of little birds, some bruised and battered but others appearing to be only asleep, though they were frozen stiff. They were mostly warblers, bright colorful blue and yellow and green and gold birds that neither of them recognized, and Jerry theorized that the storm had come in so quickly that it had caught and crashed into a migrating wave of them. Walking along the beach, they could discern now a sort of strand line, as if those birds had landed in the waves and been washed ashore, though they could not have been, for the waves of the lake were frozen mid-curl, and Jerry and Karen saw how the currents of flinging ice needles and poisonously cold air above had crushed and forced the tiny birds to the ground, where they died in a staggering line that seemed somehow nonetheless precise, with no one bird making it much farther than any of the others, and they all appeared to be strung as if on some imaginary thread, a macabre and beautiful necklace of the lake's, or the storm's, brutal making.

They had gathered the less crushed of the little birds and put them in one of their burlap bags, intending to save some of the incredible feathers. Upon returning to their cabin, they set the bag by the stove, and later in the day they heard faint cheeping. Opening the bag, they found that about half of the birds had recovered, and after releasing those, they decided not to take any feathers from the dead birds but instead chipped and chopped a large hole in the frozen ground at the edge of the great lake and buried them there, while the setting orange sun bounced its broken reflection across those opaque, frozen waves. Jerry was aware, in that moment, how strangely lucky or fortunate he felt to be standing there with Karen, and loved, and in love — how fortunate or lucky he had been to find her — and that night, their last night, they had cooked a big steak on the outdoor grill, despite the deep cold, and had each drunk a bottle of red wine, and had fallen asleep in each other's arms after murmuring the most intimate of endearments; back then, there had been no fear, no anger, no boredom — only bright newness and wonder.

Restless in the noisy little apartment at the naval base, Jerry had rolled over and thought, as if able to send some message telepathically to Karen, *Give it up, I'm not going anywhere. Wake up,* he thought, for the ten thousandth time, *wake up and come back; this is all there is.* He stared at the ceiling and listened to Jim's moans. Finally, he fell asleep briefly and dreamed an uninteresting but calming dream about one of his stone walls. In the dream, he was merely sitting there, staring at it, and feeling calmed and hopeful.

Near dawn, a long train passed near the apartment, rattling not just the windowpanes and furniture but even the floor. Jerry awoke and could feel the tingling in his bones, and wondered how that felt inside Jim's skull.

Shortly after that — Jerry had just dozed back off to sleep in the first gray light of morning — he was reawakened by the twin howls of fighter jets shrieking just overhead — Warthogs, or F-15s, piercing the sky with tremendous velocity — and, a few moments after that, a sonic boom that sounded like nothing less than the end of the world. Particles of plaster drifted in crumbles and motes from the ceiling.

Jerry got up, stiff from his night on the couch, and began making coffee. Jim emerged from his room like a bear coming out of stuporous hibernation, head tipped downward as if in penance, and sat down at the table wordlessly. Jerry asked how he was feeling, and Jim said, "Better," saying it in a way that let Jerry know he meant only better than death.

Jerry poured a cup of coffee and a glass of juice and slid them into Jim's view, the eight-inch circle of straight-downward vision between his tipped head and the tabletop, and fixed him a little bowl of yogurt and cereal, which Jim ate slowly, noisily, still staring, of necessity, at that space right in front of and beneath him. Waiting and wondering about the future, as he crunched the dry cereal, his rear teeth grinding and clacking on it like the jaw-gnashers in hell's lowest reaches.

"It's good of you to do this," Jim said. "I really appreciate it."

"It's nothing," Jerry said. "I'm glad I can help out."

Jim was more subdued that morning and allowed Jerry to lead him around by the arm and to accompany him to his checkup. While they waited for Dr. Le Page, a nurse came in and cleaned out Jim's eye, taking off the old patch and squeezing some salve into the eye — leaning over and into him like a garage mechanic working under the opened hood of a truck or car. As she leaned nearly upside down to reach him, her breasts pressing into his lowered face as she worked, it appeared that she was trying to pull his face to her chest and comfort him.

In applying the salve to his eye, the nurse dislodged the bubble slightly — Jim never felt it move, nor did his vision change in any way, but suddenly all of the pent-up tears from the previous evening came flooding from the eye like water from a hose, and watery, teary snot streamed from his nostrils, and the nurse went and got tissue. Tears kept gushing from Jim's eye, and when Dr. Le Page came in and saw this he frowned and took Jim's face in both hands and jiggled his head slightly but firmly. The bubble repositioned itself, and almost immediately the flow was shut off.

Dr. Le Page peered and probed with mirrors and special flashlights before nodding firmly and patting Jim on the back of the head.

"I did a good job on that one," he said. "I might have filled the bubble a little full, which is probably what's causing the increased discomfort you're experiencing, but I wanted to be sure. Six more days," Dr. Le Page said. "It's all going to be all right," he said. "You'll be like a new man. You won't ever see twenty-twenty out of that eye again, but your sight will return to you. It should start getting better even by the end of the week. Six more days," he said, and shook hands with them both and sent them on their way, with the morning still young and half a hundred other patients still waiting in line behind them to see him that day, and then as many the next day, and the next.

On the drive home, both men were quiet, listening to the morning radio. Jim rode with his head tipped down, concentrating on not vomiting. He wanted nothing more than to get home to his cabin, build a small fire in the stove, and sleep. If he could, he would like to sleep the whole remaining six days, and longed for some pill or prescription that would allow him to do this: to bypass the recuperative time and instead slumber away that expanse of time as would some creature hibernating beneath a dense winter shell of snow and ice.

Jerry was depressed as always by the endless bounty of strip malls that formed the fabric of the journey between Spokane and Coeur d'Alene — but finally, after a couple of hours of traffic lights, Costcos, Pizza Connections, and Kmarts, they were back into the country and heading home, and Jerry began to relax, knowing that even if he was not returning home to love, he was at least returning to beauty; as the sun rose higher, burning off the morning's valley-bottom fog, he felt again both a guilt and a gratitude for having been blessed with good eyesight.

The day seemed extraordinarily beautiful to him — the longer-rayed sunlight of early spring was so much softer and richer than had been the short blunt light of winter — and, though trying not to feel Pollyanna-ish, he took it upon himself to comment to Jim on all the beautiful things he was seeing: to be Jim's eyes for him that day. To remind Jim of all the beauty that he had to look forward to upon his recovery.

It all looked so dreamlike to him that day. An old red hay truck, goggle-eyed and coming up the road toward them, listing under the burden of immense round bales of hay. The new sunlight on the yellow straw of the hay as the truck passed. So much color.

The snowy white crown and tail of a mature bald eagle wheeling above them in the cerulean sky, framed by the emerald forest beyond.

"Would you look at that," Jerry heard himself exclaiming.

In Sandpoint, a logging truck crossed the road in front of them, loaded with such behemoths that it had taken only five logs to fill the trailer — old growth Douglas fir, with chartreuse clusters of lichens still clinging to the bark of the newly cut logs and sap still oozing from their cuts, glistening like sugar glaze in that new light.

"There's a sight you don't see every day anymore," Jerry said, referring to the size of the logs.

Jim said nothing, not even a grunt, and instead continued to ride silently, holding his aching head in his hands.

Jerry remembered what Dr. Le Page had said about the bubble's slow dissolution — how it would be absorbed into Jim's bloodstream, and then into the lungs, before being emitted as breath, as exhalation, so that Jerry was breathing in the dissolved gas of Jim's eye bubble, there in the cab of the truck.

Jim continued to ride in silence, head down, eyes squeezed shut. Jerry glanced at him and then back at the road, and tried to hold on to the sunny optimism that the day was reawakening in him.

Maybe when I get home it will be different, he thought. *Maybe she will have decided she loves me again, or that even if she doesn't, she will work toward getting to that place again. Maybe.*

He felt something shift within him, something as subtle yet significant as a cloud passing across the sun. He looked out the other window, out at the deep blue expanse of Lake Pend

Oreille. They were on the long narrow bridge that spanned its eastern harbor, heading into town from the south.

In the summer the lake was festooned with the bright flags of yachts and sailboats, but at the moment there were no boats out on its blue depths; the winter's ice still extended several hundred yards out toward the open water, still white and brilliant in some places, but in other places it was beginning to discolor back into translucent opaqueness, with mercury-colored trails of slush revealing the paths where ice fishermen had trudged earlier in the winter.

The charred stubble where their warming fires had earlier burned (bright and warm but in no way able to burn down through the thick winter-plate of ice) remained, piles of coal and stump as random and ill sorted upon the paling ice now as bones or entrails cast there by druids interested in some prophecy already gone away. It was an astoundingly lonely visage, and made more lonesome still — Jerry felt the strange thing inside him click or slip or slide further, even as if against his will — by the sight of one or two fishing huts still set up out on that waning ice; and then, somehow horrifically, he saw that some of the ice fishermen were still out there, walking out across that thinning egg-colored ice, carrying their poles and buckets and avoiding narrowly the soupy channels of disintegrating ice but pushing forward nonetheless — risking it all, risking everything, as if not out of joy but deadly habit.

From a distance, Jerry could see how dangerous it was. Already there were man-sized craters of open water out on the shelf ice, in which rested, as if in some paradoxical semblance of tranquillity, the season's first returning ducks and geese and even swans.

It wasn't just old people, either, who were streaming out to those distant huts; Jerry could see that plenty of the ice walkers were young people, young men and women walking together, still strong in their youth but certainly old enough to know better.

It was terrible to watch. Finally he couldn't stand it. Jim was dozing, having just drifted off to sleep — his head rocking up and down like a dead man's — but Jerry couldn't help it. He pulled over to the side of the road — Jim sat bolt upright for a second with the catch of fear, then remembered his instructions, and lowered his head once more — and Jerry got out of the truck and began shrieking at the distant, colorful figures making their way across the ice.

"Hey!" he shouted. "You goddamn fools! Hey! *Motherfuckers!*" he shouted, beginning to curse now for all he was worth. "Go back!" He waved at them across the distance, and a few of them stopped and stared at him, and, unable to discern his words, only his gestures, began to wave back at him.

"Go *back!*" he ranted. "Oh, you goddamned fools, go back!" But he was unable to make himself heard to them, and after a few moments of waving back to him, they drifted on farther out across the ice, leaning into the mild south wind on the bright, sunny, beautiful day, as he stood there on the bridge in full sight and continued to rant and howl.

With their backs now turned, he felt himself fading already from their consciousness — becoming as strange and irrelevant as the cold coals of their old winter-fires that lay scattered like trash across the barren, temporary snowscape.

As if, even though he stood on the bridge right before them, they could already no longer see him. As if they had chosen to no longer be able to see him.

He kept yelling, but the wind had changed now and was

carrying his words away, and they could not even hear his shouts.

The brightly colored walkers reached their huts, opened the doors, and disappeared inside. Jerry watched for a moment longer — half expecting the huts to fall through the ice — but when no tragedy ensued, he got back into the truck, where Jim, with his head still lowered, wanted to know what all the yelling had been about.

"Nothing," Jerry said. "Nothing, really. I just got scared for a minute, was all. I'm all right now. I was just scared, was all," he said. "It's okay now. It's better."

Real Town

JICK WAS UP ON the mountain gassing dogs when the windy day blew through. It was their last chance. Some chance.

He has a hank of my hair, which he bought from my ex-boyfriend after we broke up and the ex left the valley. Jick keeps the hair in a little display case in his store. He sells it for ten dollars a lock. He puts the glass box of it up by the window, so that it catches the light. It glows red. Jick knows how much it unnerves me, and he thinks I will buy it all back someday. But I don't have any money. I have to just look at it. He's sold two locks of it so far, both to tourists. People will buy anything.

He runs the store here, jacks the prices up so high that you've got to be really desperate to buy something. It's fifty miles to town, and Jick gets a not-so-secret thrill every time someone admits that paying his price is better than driving a hundred miles round trip.

Three dollars for a box of envelopes that costs next to nothing in town, in real town; a dollar for an old drying-out lemon that someone needs for a recipe; two dollars and fifty cents for a quart of milk.

It's dark in the store, and Jick's got all these skulls nailed to the log rafters with dopey little hand-lettered cardboard signs under each of them, identifying the skulls' previous owners: BEAR, RAVEN, MOUNTAIN LION, COYOTE. He's got stuffed animals on the checkout counter: blue grouse, and ruffed grouse, and a moldy weasel, tiny and lithe, with beady eyes and little whiskers that remind me so much of Jick that I sometimes feel there are two of him whenever I'm in the store. Which is not often. A gallon of gas — two bucks a gallon, versus a dollar and nine cents in real town. A six-pack of beer (don't ask!) in case friends drop in for the night. But the higher prices are about the only cost we pay for living away from real town.

It's a strange paradox: some people in the valley find themselves wanting to keep Jick in the valley, and in business — because it *is* worth it, when that lemon is needed, or a can of coffee, or a length of copper tubing, a rubber washer. Nobody up here wants to make an unnecessary trip over the pass and down the cliff road into town. So a lot of folks go by there every now and then, just to buy a little something, to try to encourage him to hang on. But then we get to feeling robbed, wasteful, after we're home, and we resolve not to go back there for another three months, or a month.

I go in there about once a year. I tell myself he can't help who he is, how he is. I get all ready to forgive and understand him. But then I see my red hair on display there and I want to cry. I feel like he's robbed me of something. Not my hair, but something invisible. Something he's too dumb to even know about.

"You're not going to be able to sell any of it," I tell him. "Please let me have it back. Please let me take it home."

I'm always angry whenever I ask him this. Because his reaction's always the same.

He smiles. A feeling of happiness comes into him. He looks glassy-eyed and eager both, like one of those people in the airport who ask you for things.

He takes his sweet time answering. He wants to engage me.

He tastes his question. I almost imagine that in a second a little forked tongue will flicker out from between his lips.

"You don't understand," he'll say. "I bought it from Walter." I'd cut Walter's hair about two or three times a year, and he'd trim mine.

"How much did Walter charge you for it?"

Jick shakes his head slowly, wall-eyed and grinning, as if disbelieving his luck, or that I don't understand the situation and the joy that red-hair-in-a-box brings him. "That's not the point," he'll say, or "That's not the right question."

Walter's long gone.

Jick putters around, fusses with stuff. He thinks, dreams, and schemes. Summer is his favorite time of year, because occasional lost tourists will wander through the valley, thinking there must be some back road up here that goes into Canada. But there's not.

Twelve dollars for camera film!

Some of Jick's putterings involve gathering elk dung — the pellets — and sticking four toothpicks into them, so that I suppose they look like some kind of cute little animal. I don't know what he thinks goes through tourists' minds. He's never sold one of those elk pellets that I know of, but still he gathers the dry elk shit in great quantities and spends a good bit of his time in the fall and winter sticking toothpicks into his herd of shit. He's got one whole shelf lined with them, near the checkout counter. His disdain for tourists, his disgust, is so obvious to the rest of us, and to them, too, I'm sure. He thinks they're dumber than he is — the worst insult of all!

Jick wanders the dry streambeds in the fall, too, picking up smooth river stones, which he carries back to his store and paints with the slogan I ♥ REAPER. Reaper is the name of our valley. They used to grow hay along the little river. Summers are real short. But it's good sweet hay. Four dollars a bale.

Some of the river rocks that Jick finds are layered silicates, algae-encrusted quartzes, agates, and opals, and whenever Jick finds one of those, he brings it home and tosses it into the big tumbling rock polisher that he keeps running in his store, twenty-four hours a day. The damn thing just runs and runs, makes a low growling sound, wearing those sleek stones down to their bare, irreducible rock core. Jick is forever pouring polishing grit — his own concoction of river and ground-up glass and motor oil — into his tumbler, and when he has each of the rocks polished, he sells it, like everything else. It seems unholy, selling part of the river itself, to passers-through. And I hate the sound, the twenty-four-hour sound, that's always growling away in his store, the stones always being worn down. You hear the stones' grinding sound whenever you walk in, and it is like the one I imagine he must hear all the time in his terrible brain.

Jick is so fucking *cheap*. There's not any electricity up here. Jick runs a big filthy Army-issue generator that throbs, like a grouse's summertime chest-drumming, all the time; when I get to within two miles of the place, I can smell the diesel. And he pisses directly into the little river that runs past his store; he stands out on his dock at night and pisses straight into the river. He's horrid.

Jick shows movies in the summer and fall, runs a projector outside under the stars, sets up a little pissant movie screen and shows films every night at dusk: horrible films like *Spiderman* and *Kung-Fu Man* and *California Dreaming*. Almost any kind of film, celluloid, flickering beneath the valley stars, would be terrible compared to the sweet brief fact of the valley and the river itself.

He's just a man. I know I shouldn't get so upset, or judgmental: he is just *one man,* in the woods — but I think I respond so strongly because I still use him, perhaps even still need him — those times when I'm low on gas, or when I want to buy a bottle of pop. He's just a little grass burr in my otherwise seamless life. I can't imagine how perfect it would be, if only he didn't — what? Exist? Is that evil? To wish him away?

Walter. Walter was a loser. There was a period there for about six months where I did not think he was a loser — and perhaps I was blind to it, or maybe, during that brief period, he really wasn't a loser — but then I could scent it. What was between us started going away, going bad — not dramatically so, but just in the usual unpleasing, unsatisfying manner — and a year or so later, he sold Jick the box of hair, which I didn't even know he'd been keeping.

Why I moved up here used to be important, but what matters now is my life right now — this day.

My mother, who lives two thousand miles away, would like a grandchild. I'm thirty-eight years old. I don't have a plan, no six-month or twelve-month or eighteen-month goal — no do or die last chance desperate hope. I'm only speaking my heart's truth, not my mind's truth: *I think I would like a child.* I have been thinking about it pretty much every day for several years now. But it probably won't happen. And I'm afraid that if I pursue it, I'd make a mistake — a big mistake.

I try to live very carefully — I try to live *right* — and I would not be comfortable rushing out and trying to change all of the years that have preceded these: trying, suddenly, to become someone I'm not. Trying to seek a man for his semen's sake, and for timeliness rather than love.

I don't have a phone, thank God. But Mother writes. She tells me that all the eggs I will ever have are already in my body, and that they have always been there, since birth. She calls them zygotes. I don't tell her that they're called eggs when they're unfertilized, and only zygotes once they've been fertilized and the embryo's growing.

She tells me that I'm losing one each month — and that someday soon I'll run out. She tells me it's like I'm bleeding to death. Great stuff.

My hair's long. I swear I'll never cut it again.

I wish the hair in Jick's glass display case would fade, or rot. But it doesn't. It's just as red and vibrant as the day it was cut. It won't ever change. The hair on my head will turn gray or silver, but the hair in that box will still be a beautiful red.

And Jick knows it. He smiles that vapid snake-smile at me whenever he sees me wanting my hair back.

I paddle a lot. I live on the river — upriver from puppy-killing Jick — but sometimes my slow drifts carry me past his store. Often, I paddle at night, because I do not like to be seen — I like to just drift and float, stroking only occasionally, and look at the night mountains.

I like the way the water sounds at night. I like the way the canoe glides, sucks, and surges. The power in my arms, the dip, pop, and pull of my shoulders. Stars fly across the mountains in cold meteor showers. Big fish, beavers, and otters lurk beneath me. Geese and ducks and mergansers cluck and gabble along the river's edge under the grassy cutbanks. It's all out there, at night. You can get closer to things, at night.

I like my life. I like it a lot.

I drift past the mercantile. That's when I've seen Jick flapping his urine into the river's clear flowing current. I've glided above the stony bottom, the current beginning to move a little faster — the falls only a few miles downstream. He represents something — my dislike for him goes beyond simple chemistry — but I don't know what it is. Some kind of stunted boundary, I think. He's always trying to *change* things.

Perhaps the strangest thing Jick does is to gather the skulls of winter-killed deer and elk. He collects them, waits until he has ten or twelve in a bag, and then puts them in a vise out in his back yard, down by the river, and goes to work on them.

He sands off the long nose-bone of the deer, and the mandibles; he sands and smoothes the cranium into a rounded shape, so that it looks like a human skull, and then he sells those in the mercantile, too, tells people that they're Indian skulls he's found, or the skulls of pioneers.

When I paddle past and see him altering those skulls, turning the bones of wild woods creatures into the skulls of humans, it sends shivers down my spine.

Some nights, passing Jick's place, I'll see he has his movie going, and there'll be six or eight or ten or twelve people out there on the lawn, under the stars, watching. There's a spot upriver where, in the night, I can come around the slow bend, beneath the great snag with the osprey's nest in it, and see all the way across the meadow, and I can see the blaze and flicker of the film being shown: I can see it like a warning, and I always turn back and paddle slowly, strongly, back upriver.

In the summer, I like to swim at night. The water's warmer. I like to go on a long hike, hiking through the woods all afternoon, and then come back down to the river at dusk and undress. I like to float downstream on my back, and then turn over and swim back upstream, and then float back down, watching the darkening sky and the bats and the stars. I'll do this again and again; swim upstream, then float downstream a couple hundred yards, swim back upstream, to my cabin, then float back downstream, watching the mountains. During my period, I let myself slough off and away, into the river.

One egg per month. All the eggs I will ever have are already in me. I release one per month. But I am not bleeding to death.

On the windy day, which was like no day any of us had ever seen before, we found ourselves gathering outside the mercantile. Jick has a radio with a big antenna rising from the roof of his store, and he can run it off his generator and pick up stations as far away as Spokane, which was where the last big fire started, sixty years ago — the one that burned all the way to Whiteflesh before stopping at the Fishgut River. We knew Jick would probably charge us fifty cents each for listening to the news on his radio, but it was where we all began to show up, to check in with each other — outside his store. We had to bring our saws with us to cut paths through the trees that kept blowing over and falling across the road in the high winds. There was smoke and ash blowing everywhere. It seemed quite possible at the time that it was the end of the world. We didn't know if it was a huge forest fire to the west, or a volcano, or nuclear fallout. No one was melting the way I understood happened with nuclear attacks, and we've always kind of believed, anyway, in our deepest hearts, I think, that our valley would be exempt from all that stuff: that not even *that* could reach us up here.

Jick wasn't in; he was up on the mountain. Someone had

given him a box full of sled dog puppies to gas. Jick performs that service for a dollar a pup, and some people, when they have to get rid of their dogs, take the dogs to Jick just to avoid the guilt, or bad karma, or to keep from upsetting the kids.

Too many times, I've seen Jick's truck heading slowly up that mountain.

He drives all the way up to the mountaintop: not for any spiritual reason, I'm sure, but simply because that's how far all the roads on the mountains in this valley go — to the top — and also because, I'm afraid, he savors the ride.

Thinking about it. About gassing those pups. About keeping his world exactly the way it is — exactly the way he wants it.

People talk about Jick's dog-killing, make jokes about him behind his back — about how he sits up there with his truck idling, looking down over the valley, over the blotchy griddle-squares of sweep-away clearcuts. He has a dryer hose that he can hook from his truck's muffler to go directly into this gassing box he's rigged up. People joke about how he sits up there with his aviator sunglasses on and scans the valley below and hums, listening to some tape in his tape deck. He must feel the truck vibrating, idling, and perhaps he thinks about how the pups are writhing and coughing, and then, finally, settling into sleep, lying down all on top of each other in that gassing box, up on top of the mountain.

Several of my friends, back in real towns, have had abortions. Two have had miscarriages. I have had neither.

Sometimes I feel like fresh meat, waiting. I feel like yielding, like giving myself up to it. Sometimes, I want it. But only sometimes.

We were all standing around the store in the swirling smoke, waiting for him to come back down with the dead pups. The strange strong wind kept knocking trees down across the road. We could hear Jick's chainsaw up on the mountain as he tried to work his way back down, clearing away the wind-felled trees, and I knew he was hating those pups for the mess they'd gotten him into.

Because the mercantile was locked, we had to wait outside his door. There's one pay phone outside his store, one phone line coming in from a smaller town downriver, but that line had long ago gone dead.

There was so much smoke in the parking lot that it was hard to see one another. I saw my friend Mary and her husband, Joe, and moved over to stay close to them.

The smoke just kept getting thicker and thicker. It was green smoke. Deer were running down the streets like horses, panicked, and I remembered the movie *Bambi* from when I was a child, from when I was growing up. I wondered if the circle of childbearing was going to end, if I would be the one to stop that circle: to step slightly to the side, and let childhood, in our family, stop.

I couldn't see that far at all, in all that smoke. Cars and trucks kept gliding in, appearing through the smoke with their headlights blazing, creeping down the road — deer, and one moose, running ahead of them — and everyone was gathering at the only place we knew to gather, the mercantile.

No one had heard anything. Our radios never picked up anything but static and crackle in the valley, even under the best conditions. Mary and I stood next to the window. We could see my hair in the display case. It looked like it was waiting for something. I felt separated from something. It would have pleased me, I think, in that moment, for the whole valley to have burned down: if only the hair would burn with it.

We stood around, made braver by one another's presence — some people smiling thin smiles — and finally we saw Jick's headlights moving toward us from out of the smoke and wind.

He took up a collection to start the generator, explaining that it had been through a lot of wear and tear lately. Some of us had money and some didn't. Mary gave Jick a dollar.

If the radio told us to evacuate, I don't know if we would have or not. Sue and Bill had their two boys with them, as well as the baby; Sue stayed in the truck with a wet handkerchief over the baby's mouth, while Bill and the boys stood outside and scuffed their boots at the ground and listened as Jick brought his radio out on the porch.

I saw one of Bill's boys go over to the back of Jick's truck and stare at the dead puppies, which were all stretched out neatly, soft and gray. I saw the boy pat one of the dead puppies, stroking its head. I think a little boy would be nice. I know I'd like a little girl.

A girl!

The radio squelched and whistled, crackled and drifted. Finally, Jick found a station — a country music station. A song by Charley Pride was playing. We stood there in the smoke and listened to that, waiting for it to be over, and when it was, another song came on.

Jick turned the tuner and found another station — a bunch of commercials — and then when the commercials were over, a disc jockey came on and said that he was going to play twelve in a row.

We found a news station, finally, near the end of the dial, but there wasn't any mention of fires, or about our valley burning up, or any other kind of disaster. More music began to play instead.

People began to grumble and stir, moving back toward their trucks. I think we all felt both endangered and protected, isolated and yet safe. If it had been real bad, I reasoned, then the people in real town would have been coming for us, trying to save us.

Still, there was the knowledge that the fires could be very close, and that we could all burn up overnight.

Maybe people in real town didn't know what was going on up here!

We certainly couldn't get out of the valley. We were locked in by all the thousands of wind-felled, and wind-falling, trees — by the forest collapsing on itself, the younger trees without deep roots getting blown over like grass, offering no fight at all, nothing but fodder for the forest floor.

I must live right, I thought, driving home slowly — getting out to cut several more trees out of my way, and watching carefully through the smoke for more falling trees. *If I get through this,* I thought, *I will live even more strongly than ever* — though I was not frightened, and it was not the foxhole kind of promise one often makes in such times of danger.

This day, the windy day — the day Jick came driving in with all those gassed baby pups — it was more like just a simple vow, and a positive thing. I felt good about my vow: *I will live harder.*

Sometimes I'd like an omen, about what I should do. But there aren't any. Nature's rarely that way. Nature's slow, and we're quick. If the windy day had been an omen, I can't imagine what kind. I think it was just a windy day.

The next day there was less smoke, and by the day after

that it had all cleared. It was just the smoke from some grass fires over in Idaho, carried over into our valley on the high winds.

Not far downriver from me, there is a married couple, Greg and Beth, who are expecting their first child in the spring. They're not all that much younger than I — in their early thirties — and sometimes on my early-morning canoe rides I go along the river right past their cabin. They sleep later than I do; smoke does not begin to rise from their chimney until after daylight. I see all kinds of creatures on my canoe rides — deer by the dozens, and coyotes, ravens, and moose, bull elk, and porcupines, and once a pair of mountain lions. Sometimes I will stop outside of Greg and Beth's cabin, about a hundred yards off, hidden back in the cottonwoods and the tall frosted cattails, and will study the still-ness of their cabin: the way nobody's moving, the way nobody's up and about yet. Sometimes I imagine how it must be for Beth in there, sleeping, warm beneath the blankets, with that baby warm inside her. I sit there in my canoe and wait for the sun to come up — for it to strike my hair with red, to set it aflame.

Sometimes I'll get out and walk along the shore. There are interesting tracks in the mud along the riverbank: cranes, her-ons, and other wading and shore birds.

There's supposed to be a real nice man up here, a biologist, a young man, not too far down valley. I suppose I should go and visit him, but I'm scared. I'd like to wait just a little longer.

Birds rise from the river's marsh grasses, the tall cattails, and take frantic flight as I move along the river's edge. A beaver slips up from the bulrushes, dives into the still pond above its dam of chewed-up sticks: dives deep, plunging.

I keep walking, scaring up more birds: killdeer, snipe, and plover. They fly away fast and do not come back.

Eating

SOMETIME BEFORE DAWN, on their first date, driving north through North Carolina to go canoeing in the mountains, they hit an owl. Sissy was sitting up, leaning against Russell's shoulder, and they had been listening to the radio, not speaking, benumbed by the lateness of the hour and the endless roll of road beneath.

They saw the underside of the owl flare up, brilliant white in the glare of the headlights — it swooped right at their faces, barely missing the windshield — and then there was half an instant of silence, so that they thought they had missed it (it was a great horned owl, and seemed as large and incongruous to the night sky in that brief moment as a flying man), but then they heard and felt the thump of the large body striking the canoe, and a few feathers swirled past their windshield, and after slowing and looking back, not seeing it, they drove on, remorseful, saddened.

"Maybe he made it," Russell said.

They followed narrow winding mountain roads that hugged steep cliffs and the edges of rivers, from which rose ribbons of steam. They drove slower and slower, and saw more and more owls, passing through them as if through a nighttime hatch of immense moths, though they didn't strike any more.

They were still in North Carolina when the sun came up, burning orange-red through the fog, and they stopped for breakfast at a small diner that had a smokehouse attached to its side, through the wood-slat cracks of which issued slow blue smoke. The scent of the smoke caught their attention as if a clothesline had been strung across the road.

The diner was built from old cinder blocks and the parking lot was red clay with scattered beds of gravel. Numerous low swales held muddy water. The lot was filled with old mud-splattered trucks and cars, bald-tired and with sprung-out taillights and headlights duct taped in place. All of the license plates were local, and none of the vehicles had bumper stickers of any kind — as if the drivers led lives so pure as to be unconcerned of anything beyond their immediate control.

Russell and Sissy went out back first to take a look at what was cooking. They found glistening pork ribs and ham steaks blushing as red as oak leaves in autumn. Some chickens, too.

"I'm hungry," Russell said. They stood there in the blue smoke, letting it bathe them for a while, and looked out at the forest dropping away below them: sweetgum, hickory, oak, loblolly, mountain laurel. They could see more ridges, more knolls and valleys, gold lit, through the framework of green leaves and branches. Tobacco country, down in the lowlands. Russell took another look at the hams. "This is my country," he said. "Or getting real near it."

He turned and studied the mound of fresh-split oak sitting next to the grill. Fuel for the coming day's work of altering the taste of a thing. He didn't possess a trace of fat. It would be hard to guess where the calories went on him. It was his own opinion that they just sort of vaporized, like coal or some other combustible shoved into a glowing furnace.

When they went inside, the diners all swiveled to study them unabashedly, and at length. Sissy had never felt so on display. Old farmers in blue denim overalls and straw hats staring at her through Coke-bottle glasses. Canes. Gap-teeth, gold teeth, tobacco teeth. Finally Sissy felt compelled to speak. "Hello," she said.

One of the old farmers gestured the nub of a finger toward Russell, and then toward their car, and toward the canoe perched atop it.

"Son," he said, "what are you doin' with that owl?"

They looked out the window and saw that an owl, bent-looking and ruffled, was sitting on the hood of their car, blinking. It had gotten sucked up into the canoe, and Russell had been driving so fast it must have ridden pinned back in the stern, unable to get out. Now that the car had stopped and the pressure had been released, the owl seemed scarcely able to believe it was free.

"Can it fly?" one of the old men asked. Others were staring at Russell now.

"We must have scooped it out of the sky," Russell said.

Only about half of them believed him. They set their papers down and sipped their coffee and watched the owl with interest and speculation. "It seems disinclined to fly," one of the men said.

"Hit's watching us back," said another, and now it seemed as if a gauntlet had been laid down, so that there was no way the old men would let the owl — this ruffled, yellow-eyed interloper — out-stare them, and they crouched forward, leaning over their steaming cups of coffee, and surveyed the owl, which was still squatting in similar fashion, hunch-shouldered, as suspicious of the events that had brought him to this place as were the old men.

Sissy and Russell settled in to eat: road-weary and ravenous, they settled slowly, firmly, back into the real world. Russell could not decide what to exclude from the menu, so he ordered one of everything — pancakes, grits, ham, fried eggs, ribs, bacon, biscuits, gravy — and as if to counterbalance his gluttony, Sissy ordered a cup of coffee and a thin piece of ham.

They ate in silence. A slash of morning sunlight fell across their table, and, after so much darkness on their drive through the night, the sunlight seemed now to carry extra sweetness and clarity.

Russell finished his first helpings and decided to focus thereafter on the fried eggs and ham. The waitress brought him another plate and he stretched — the cracking of tight ligaments in his back sounded almost musical — and told the waitress she'd better just start frying eggs, and that he'd tell her when to stop.

One of the old men noticed the new plate of food and marked a little tally of it on his napkin.

Russell ate steadily for over half an hour: two eggs, ham, two eggs, ham. The restaurant ran out of eggs after he had eaten twenty-four, though they still had some ribs and ham left; but finally Russell said he had had enough, and he leaned back and stretched and patted, then thumped, the taut skin of his belly.

He reached out and took Sissy's hand fondly, and they sat there for a while alongside the old men, in the mild sunlight, and watched the owl.

"Hit wants in to eat some ham, too," one of them speculated.

"If a cat walks by, that owl'll kill it," another warned, and now they began to look about almost eagerly, hoping for such a drama.

As if bored by *not* eating, Russell decided to order a single pancake for dessert, and when it arrived he doused it with syrup and then ate it slowly, with much satisfaction, and said, "Damn, I wish I had an egg to go on top of this," and the old men laughed.

Russell finished and then got up to go to the bathroom. The waitress got on the phone and began ordering reinforcements for the larder. Sissy noticed that the phone was an old black rotary dial and felt again that they had driven into the past. The old men asked Sissy where they were from, and when Sissy said "Mississippi" the old men looked slightly troubled, as if concerned that there might be more coming just like them: invaders, insatiable infidels — a population of marauders who might devour the entire town.

In the bathroom, Russell settled in on the toilet and stared out the open window at the garden beyond. The lace curtains fluttered in the morning breeze. As Russell was gazing, a mule's enormous head appeared from out of nowhere, startling him considerably. The mule looked as if he had come to inspect something, and, not knowing what the mule wanted, Russell handed him one end of the roll of toilet paper, which the mule took in his enormous teeth and then walked away carefully, gently, drawing the toilet paper out in a steady unspooling.

Russell watched, mesmerized, as the mule wandered randomly around the garden and through the field and then around the corner, around toward the front of the restaurant, as if laying down the borders of some newly claimed territory — and it was not until the spool of paper was nearly unwound that Russell had the presence of mind to snap it off and save some for himself.

When he emerged, the old men and the waitress were staring at him as if wondering what he might do next, and he and

Sissy went out and began gathering the toilet paper, even as the mule now moved along behind them, grazing on the paper.

At first the owl would not let them near their car, hissing and snapping at them, but Russell got a branch and was able to dislodge it; they watched as it launched itself hale and hearty into silent flight, and disappeared, a hunter, into the woods. They waved goodbye to the old men and the waitress and drove off, and as they were leaving the parking lot they saw another truck turning in, a beat-up old red truck carrying in the back of it a single immense hog, which looked none too excited about the journey, as if knowing — maybe from the odor of the smokehouse — what stage of life's journey he was now entering.

"Are you always like this?" Sissy asked as they drove on farther, deeper into the mountains, anticipating the day.

"Like what?" Russell asked.

The Distance

1

WHEN MASON WAS sixteen, he traveled with a group of Explorer Scouts from Texas to all the great cultural landmarks along the East Coast, including Monticello. He remembers precious little from that trip and those long days. The fetid odor from the Greyhound bus's toilet, a disgusting mix of urine, feces, and antiseptic. A ravenous hunger for junk food. The incessant crunching of Doritos from every youth on the bus, at any and all hours — mandibles clacking as if a brigade of giant insects was on the move. A dull, pervasive homesickness — his first trip of any distance or length — that was at times overwhelming.

Of the grounds at Monticello, and the great house that was a dream made real, Mason remembers almost nothing, save for the vague and uneasy sense that Jefferson had been a crackpot, quite possibly a loser, or at best a bully — trying to impose his rigid principles on everybody around him.

Everyone kept raving about what a marvelous structure Monticello was, so democratic and modern, etc., but to Mason it just looked old and used-up, awkward and boring. Mason was neither strong nor smart for his age, and for much of the first twenty-five years or so of his life it seemed to him that he slept not just at night but through the days. Later in his life, the love of an exciting woman, different from any he had ever known, would be the one thing that most awakened him. But from that time, that trip to Monticello, he can't even remember if it was raining or if the sun was shining.

Only the perpetual smell of the toilet, mixed with the diesel fumes each time the bus would slosh forward from a stoplight. The crunching of the Doritos.

The steady homesickness. The first hint of the feeling that something hugely important — the great and vast reservoir of the essence of time itself, previously unerodable — was beginning, slowly and finally, to be consumed. A few days of his life, just a few but for the first time ever being nibbled away, as the ocean washes away at the sand grains poised at the edge of the tide's far reach.

2

It's been more than a quarter of a century, but now Mason finds himself back at Monticello, at the age of forty-two, in the company of that woman who helped awaken him and their two daughters, just-turned eight and five. Mason and his family live in Montana now, east of Great Falls, in the prairie, where Mason is a schoolteacher. It's spring break, and in Virginia, at Monticello, the sun is shining.

Huge dragon-headed clouds tower in an azure sky, and nine-masted schooners plow in all directions the eternal blue, trailing in their wake schools of leaping porpoises. Any thought that ever crossed a person's mind is represented in the towering swirl of clouds, this fine spring day. Anything a person wants to see can be found there in the sky, this beautiful breezy day.

After a winter of squabbling, the girls are playing, for the first time in a long time, like little angels; as if in that mild spring breeze some spirit is passing through the high branches of the great trees planted by the hand of the distant gentleman himself, so long ago. How he had wanted to control his world, and, for a little while, how he had succeeded. Jefferson had kept pet mockingbirds that were trained to fly in and out of his open windows. He had once owned a semidomesticated bull elk that would wander the grounds, not too tame and yet not too wild, either, moving along always in that blurred perimeter between the groomed orchard and the deeper woods, moving gracefully in that last wedge of each day's waning light and sliding-in dusk: the elk in that manner seeming poised perfectly between the land of dreams and the land of the specific, the knowable.

Historians say that for much of Jefferson's later life, after the first elk vanished, he kept hoping to train another elk to fill that space, and those crepuscular moments, in the same fashion, but he was never again quite successful; all the other elk either became too tame, wandering up onto the porches even in the broad light of day, hoping for handouts, or were too wild, bolting for the deep woods immediately upon being released, and never being seen again.

How his precisionist's heart must have raged against this fluidity, this refusal to adhere specifically to his ironclad plans and schemes. He died on the fourth of July, fifty years after he and his peers had penned the Declaration of Independence — lingering on his deathbed for weeks, it is said, in order to make it to that anniversary — and yet Mason has to wonder if in his last moments Jefferson was not remembering any declarations scripted, but instead dreaming yet again of that mythic antlered beast, the one whose force he wished to harness and whose dim blue shadow he had been able to glimpse out his window at that one and perfect hour, each dusk, striding just barely in sight through the trees and the failing light, at the far and outer reaches of reality, less than a bound, a step, away from the land of dreams. A messenger, each evening, between that world and this one.

Other failures — things he could not control — included the growth of trees and the grapes in his vineyard. Any guidebook will tell the reader what a genius the man was (inventor, statesman, writer, politician, gentleman farmer), but again, secret folly: the red clay atop that lovely hill would not nurture domestic grapes, only the native wild Mustang variety — his imports from his beloved France failed, and failed, and failed (two hundred years later, vineyards in the region would learn to graft the French bodies on to the native roots, and in that manner, finally, make passable wine); and it was another of his great and hidden frustrations that the trees he planted as an old man would never mature in his lifetime.

"If I could beseech favor from an opportune heaven," he wrote in his eightieth year, "it would be to live to see the sight of these trees I have planted fully mature, their leaves brilliant in autumn, bare and elegant in winter, lush emeralds in spring, and deep-shaded during the shimmering roar of summer."

He declared that the cutting of stately trees was an act "nothing less than murder," and he built at the edge of his vast vegetable garden a tiny lighthouse overlooking the Shenandoah Valley, so that after each evening's gardening he could sit in that little glass turret, wine glass in hand, and stare at, and be calmed by, the lithe and supple folds of those endless blue hills, the fog hanging in folds and crevices far below him and the mountains seeming to move slowly away, like the slow waves upon a faraway ocean.

All of his frustrations were hidden; history was kind to him, and chance and forgetfulness were his flatterers. His errors and failures have not traveled the same distance as his successes.

He wanted to have weeping willows lining the path of the stone walk that led down to his family's cemetery, where, among others, his father, the mapmaker, was buried. Jefferson invented a form of drip irrigation that kept the plants watered well enough during the few years he had remaining that they were able to stay alive, though they grew slowly and died not long after he died; it was simply not the right kind of country for them. Untenable. Even now, however, according to his wishes, the managers of his estate plant new willows every few years in the thin clay soil along that graveyard walk, on that hill that is too steep for willows — pulling up the old dead ones that always grow too far beyond their nutrients like an outsized mind hungering, starving for stimulation but finding none.

Each year's plantings never come close to reaching the cool and elegant heights envisioned by their dreamer, though still, two hundred years later, his acolytes persist, as if hoping or believing even now, and still, that the dream might take hold.

Luck attended him almost always; he hid his failures and frustrations so well that perhaps he forgot he had them; in that manner, the failures were released and perhaps truly did depart. Where the vineyards languished after his death, wild hollyhocks, iris, and roses grew, as did orchards of apples, plums, and pears.

It was almost a hundred years after his death before a scholar found, in the depths of his thousands of pages of private journals and correspondence, his blue dream of that strange elk, existing always in that perfect distance between the hearth and the ravening, ungovernable wilderness.

Where the garden would not grow blueberries, he planted

asparagus and kale. The ghostlike, almost translucent leaves of the latter bloomed wildly beneath the overturned clay pots that encased the plants like crypts — again, such a gardening method was one of his many inventions — the eternal darkness rendering the vegetables' milk-colored flesh (the color of a blind cave-creature, beneath those pots, sweating in the Virginia sun) as crisp as crackers.

He ate meat very sparingly, only a thin bite or two every now and again, using it not as a staple but as a condiment to accent or supplement the taste of the vegetables from his garden. A rabbit might last him in that manner a fortnight; a venison ham, a whole year. The great elk itself, two or three lifetimes, had he deigned to kill it.

Mason's wife is an artist. She has an artist's temperament, even more so than does Mason, who likewise seems too often to be passing back and forth too wildly between the fields of peace and the fields of war, between elegant self-control and passionate recklessness, between heaven and hell, between beauty and agony. This one fine afternoon, though, things are not as bad as they often are, which is as if one or both of them has been wounded — a musket ball shattering a foreleg, a piercement of the lungs, and a crooked, wandering spattering trail of blood wherever they go, with no pleasant outcome in sight able to be forecast by either themselves or anyone who knows them.

(The children, the children, what is to become of the children?)

Again and again, Mason and Alice keep telling themselves — after each setback — that they will try harder, that they will not give up.

This day, however — this shining afternoon — for some

reason, exhaustion perhaps, they are not fighting, and Alice is sitting by Mason's side, holding his arm with both hands like a young bride, and they are watching their two young daughters roll down the hill like logs, clasping each other's hands like acrobats as they laugh and shout and roll down the steep green manicured lawn: to the bottom, back up to the top; to the bottom, back up to the top. It feels, in the peace and happiness of the moment, as if Alice and Mason in their chronic unhappiness have somehow — perhaps through the miracle of endurance, or even luck; surely not through any ingenuity — pierced some thin but resistant membrane that has heretofore separated them from such happiness.

The sun is warm upon their skin.

The girls are lying midslope, heads on each other's shoulders, warm wind ruffling their beautiful hair. The oldest is sketching in her journal a portrait not of the dome of Monticello — ignoring it much as Mason had, so long ago — but instead of the slave quarters, which lie behind them.

The five-year-old watches her big sister with both raptness and pleasure — in the younger sister's eyes, the eight-year-old can do no wrong. The eight-year-old takes after her mother and is a great artist with the knack for reproducing things exactly as they are. The light on the old red bricks of the quarters (brick that was baked on the premises, the slaves gathering the raw red earth in buckets and then shaping it into the bricks that would later imprison them, so that in that strange manner it was somehow as if the earth itself, upon which they lived, in whose gardens they grubbed and hoed, and at whose red hillsides they now clawed, was imprisoning them; as if their imprisonment were being rendered by the movement of their own two hands, each of them, if not by their hearts' or minds' will) — is striking the bricks in yellowish slants, and the two colors, the yellow sunlight and the red bricks, ignite each other so that the whole structure is glowing, with both colors thus accentuated.

The old lilacs that shroud the slave quarters are drooping purple and sugar-scented over those glowing red bricks, and tourists are walking back and forth in low murmuring conversations. Mason and Alice's daughters continue to lie in the center of the lawn, one sketching earnestly, the other admiring her. Mason and Alice are sitting farther up the hill, halfway between the slave quarters and the girls, looking down upon the girls, and Mason has to wonder if the oldest is sketching them, too.

Is it of note to mention again that their marriage after twenty years has foundered; that the river of not just love but even simple care and compassion has run all but dry, and that too many days now they stumble as if blind through their lives with confusion and lack of resolve or commitment — they, who were once so strong?

It doesn't matter. This day, this one day with the girls, their precious masters, lying together farther down the hill, shoulder to shoulder, their hair tousled by the wind, Mason and Alice seem to be drawn along, for once — or for the first time in a long time — all of them drawn along, parents and children alike, as if on some idyllic, gliding sleigh. As if the world has been created for their pleasure, so that they might participate in its many sharp beauties; and as if, though in the not-too-distant past they have gotten lost or sidetracked from that mission, they have now wandered back onto the path and been found again.

As if the simple sight of their oldest daughter sketching in her journal — as if constructing some master plan for something — is enough to bring them back into the world, and back onto the path of love.

Doesn't anyone, everyone, after twenty years of sameness,

encounter such crises? Aren't we all extraordinarily frail and in the end remarkably unimpressive, creatures too often of boring repetition and habit rather than bold imagination?

Who will rescue us, if not ourselves? Who will emancipate us, if not ourselves?

There is no one among us, Mason thinks, who does not dream of that wild elk. There is no one who is not, in some part, to some degree, both the animal itself — torn between wanting to slip off down farther into the dark wilderness, and back up into the clean lawns and orchards of the tame, the possessed, the cared-for — and yet also the viewer rather than the elk — the watcher who waits and watches and hungers for that elk.

Eyes staring, right at dusk, for movement right at the edge of the great woods.

Waiting, right at dusk, for that lift of heart, upon first seeing the great beast take its first step from out of the impenetrable, magnificent wilderness.

3

The tour guide stands before their group in the first great room to the north of the Rotunda and stares unseeing through the gathered and waiting throng separated from her by a velvet rope.

She stands poised like a diver perched at the top of a high platform, arms raised aloft in a flamelike taper, unblinking. She appears to be in her mid-fifties, still high-cheekboned, her hair still red-tinged, cut neat and short. Her eyes seem to glitter with an anger, the source of which the tour members cannot at first place, but slowly, it comes to Mason: she is angry that Mr. Jefferson is dead. She is in love with Mr. Jefferson.

Three tours per hour, thirty people per tour, eight hours a

day, five days a week: she testifies to her love for the man to 180,000 people per year, face to face.

She tells them right up front that he was a genius. "He loved to build clocks," she says. "His mind was like a clock. Here we see a Swiss clock that Mr. Jefferson designed and built by his own hand," she says, gesturing to an immense contraption resting directly above the entranceway like a gargoyle or some instrument of torture: huge and iron-laden enough to take flight, like some primitive flying machine.

Various chains and pulleys hang from it in all directions, with iron balls of varying sizes weighting each chain with just the right tension so as to perfectly pull all the cogs and gears in the precise manner necessary to keep perfect time. "It hasn't missed a minute in over two hundred years," the guide says proudly. As if she had been around during the building of it and might have somehow participated.

"The clock was designed so that it would inform one not only of the hour of the day, but of the day of the week. However, the balls on the lowermost chains, which drove Saturday and Sunday, ran out of room and got tangled on the floor, so Mr. Jefferson cut a hole in the floor through which the chains could pass into the basement." A sweep of her hand toward the saw notch in the corner, which indeed does swallow the ball and chains. A tiny, chaste smile. Her waist is pinched tight, and she wears an elegant long velour dress. Her eyes are bright, damp. Eighteen minutes to go. She moves like a metronome, aware of where she stands each second of her time remaining, the audience's time remaining. The time remaining in the story itself.

She ushers the group into the next room, the library. She walks backwards as she speaks, keeping the narrative running; she pirouettes in just the right place to fold herself into a little cleft to allow the others to flow into the small curved room. Some part of her beholds them as the lion tamer with his whip and chair might behold the lion: somewhat frightened of, but also attracted to, their hunger.

"Here are his boots," she says, pointing, as if he might have pulled them off only last night. "Here is his writing table," she says, "where he stood by this window and composed music. As you can see by the height of the table," she says, "he was a tall man — six foot two and a quarter. Very elegant, very graceful, even into old age." The faintest touch of a smile.

Another flourish, quarter turn, and sweep to the left: dancing with his ghost as if at some grand cotillion, chin held high, her eyes sparkling now. A gesture to the wall of olden books in the library. (Has she read them all? Doubtless, and by candlelight — her fingertips resting lightly on the pages upon which his hands, too, had rested. The flames flickering, and roughly the same thoughts and images passing from those pages into her mind as passed into his, until she is so close to him — almost there — that it seems surely he will come around the corner at any moment; that he has simply been gone for a while and will be coming home soon, with the evening late, and weary from so long a journey.)

"Books were very rare, very expensive, in Mr. Jefferson's day," she tells them. "As you can see, however, he valued them highly, felt them to be the highest form of democracy — free speech coupled with the rational, considered, crafted expression of intellect. He was a prodigious reader, almost insatiable." Her lips glisten slightly at this last word, and she begins to warm to her audience, sharing her man with them, relaxing visibly as she feels them growing into his admirers as well.

"Knew seven foreign languages fluently. Taught himself Spanish in twenty days, en route to that country in 1791. Departed the shores of this country on his voyage not knowing a word of it, and landed in Spain speaking it like a native.

"He was a connoisseur of fine wines, and as prodigious a correspondent as he was a reader." A sidelong, almost sultry slipping into his study, which adjoins his bedroom. "He scribed over twenty thousand letters in his lifetime, writing to friends and family and statesmen around the world.

"Notice the contraption perched above his desk," she instructs them — another elegant arrangement of chains and pulleys, leverage and manipulation. A blank writing tablet on the other side of the desk, and an iron claw gripping a fountain pen at that tablet, so that as Mr. Jefferson sat at his desk and wrote, the iron claw of the ghost-grip seated at the table across from him would mirror his movements, reproducing his letter in duplicate, complete with every little nuance of script.

"Thus are his records preserved," says Mr. Jefferson's lover. "Another of his many inventions." A pause, as if winded. Her heart — and, she is pleased to see, those of many in her audience, now — fluttering. She might as easily at this point climb up on the desk and shout through cupped hands: "They just don't make men like they used to!"

"Here, his bedroom," she says simply, pausing for the briefest of moments — the bare requisite minimum — and pointedly avoiding looking at the tiny bed (which does not appear as if it could have housed a man of six foot two and one quarter), gazing instead fixedly at the fireplace. One of her hands trembles slightly, but her voice remains steady. He is far away, it is true, but it is also true he can travel no farther; the distance will get no worse than this. She can hold steady from this point on. She can endure.

"Here, his telescope, through which he could keep up with the distant daily progress on the construction of one of his pet projects, the groundbreaking for the University of Virginia. An avid and learned astronomer, as well. Of course."

Light comes in through the ancient curved windows through glass that Mr. Jefferson ordered from England — he sent out the dimensions, complete with trigonometric taper and calculated arc and radius; waited a year for the glass to be custom made and carried home across the swirling, tempestuous ocean. Imagine, please, his shuddering delight when that English glass finally made its way to him, when the carpenters lifted it carefully from the wagon, uncrated it intact, and held it gently, lovingly, up to the frames, fitting each piece into its waiting frame. It seems to be a tired but beautiful light, wavering green and gold, as if transmitting not just sunlight but also the botanical exuberance of the gardens outside — the dream, the vision, of Monticello.

On the tourists' arms and faces this old light seems subaqueous and calming, as if they have entered into some finer, stiller place, where their full potential, their dreams and aspirations, can still be achieved, and are but a day, or even only a moment, away.

The guide seems suddenly tired, and why not, for what could be more exhausting than waiting for a thing that's never going to come?

"Complex times," she says simply, jarring the tourists' thoughts back to her world, to Mr. Jefferson's. "He said that slavery was an abomination to the Lord, even though he remained a slaveowner all his life. He said that he trembled at the thought of this country's fate when he considered that his Lord was a just Lord." The tiniest of shrugs, and, despite a sadness of expression, a brave nonchalance in her voice almost approaches a lilt. "One of his slaves, Sally Hemings, bore a child that carried Jefferson family DNA," she says. One of the audience members is up to date on the scandal and whispers loudly that the father couldn't have been any of Jefferson's brothers, as they were all out of the country at the time the conception would have occurred. The guide's eyes glitter and flash, but she ignores the blasphemer. On to the next room.

"We know that he loved trees, forests," she says. "All of nature. A fine and eloquent writer, as well." She closes her eyes with an expression that seems to suggest she is recalling last night's kisses.

"His *Notes on the State of Virginia,* initially a response to a questionnaire sent to him in 1780 by Francois Marbois, then the secretary to the French legation in Philadelphia, is one of our most remarkable documents from the age of Enlightenment and remains one of the most influential scientific books ever written by an American." She squeezes her eyes shut tighter, continues to murmur his praises like a dove cooing or a breeze moving quietly through the boughs of tall pines.

"His was a remarkable blending of scientific and literary sensibilities. He was one of the first philosophers to argue for the concept we know now as 'biodiversity,' when he stated: 'We must learn to accept that not all beauty exists primarily to serve our hungers, but can exist on its own grounds. The earth contains not less than thirty or forty thousand kinds of plants; not less than six or seven hundred of birds; nor less than three or four hundred of quadrupeds; to say nothing of the thousand species of fishes. Of reptiles and insects, there are more than can be numbered. To all these must be added the swarms and varieties of animalcules and minute vegetables not visible to the natural eye, but whose existence is surely reciprocal with those of the greater beings.'

"'On comparing this vast profusion of life and multiplicity of beings with the few grains and grasses and livestock of those species immediately serviceable to the wants of man, it is difficult to understand the compulsion within us to erase or remodel every work of nature by a destruction not only of individuals, but of entire species; and not only of a few species, but of every species that does not seem to serve our immediate accommodations.'

"'All wilderness has beauty. And from that beauty, worth on its own accord.'"

The guide pauses, as if remembering days she spent with Mr. Jefferson, youthful days, days in a love nearly as deep as the one she possesses for him now. She pauses, casts her eyes to the soft hills of the horizon. "'The Tulip Tree,' she says, recalling more of his text. "'It creates astonishment, in the spring, to behold trees of such a magnitude, bearing a flower for a fortnight together in its shape, size, and color resembling tulips. In some places these marvelous leaves possess the appellation of a woman's smock.'" A glance to the east garden. "'And the dogwood: among the curious plants growing in our wilderness, none contribute more to the beauty of the springtime than the delightful dogwood. Our natives have the custom of tying a flowering branch of this tree around the cattles' neck, when they fall down exhausted by heat in the summer, imagining that its redolent odor and other ornamental virtues contributes to their recovery.'

"'In all, our wild forests will continue surely to be one of our nation's greatest treasures and sources of strength, and will provide with their grace and might a durable example of proper moral fiber and endless inspiration. The men who oversee their destruction for the quickness of profit are no better than murderers, in my account.'"

Which brings her to the Lewis and Clark room. More gold light seeping in through those old and molten windows, and just outside the curved glass, the elegant leaves of an Osage orange, brought back by the intrepid voyagers on their return from the Great West — a place Mr. Jefferson had always wanted to visit but never saw.

The guide has permission to open those ancient windows, and she does so with such care that it is as if she is taking a sacrament. The scent of spring floats in, as does true sunlight now, and the children as well as the adults stir and lift their sleepy heads, are refreshed, invigorated again, as if some great and living personage — not dusty history and bygone greatness — has just entered the room.

It would be impossible to overestimate how deeply in love Mason and Alice once were. Suffice it to say that the velocity and mass of it were enough to carry them even on momentum alone to this point and place, still loyal and conjoined, twenty years later.

It was like a tsunami originating far out at sea, and still the shore, and the flattening of the tide, has not yet been reached, though surely they can see the shore now and can take in the scent of olive branches and citrus groves, apple orchards and meadows; the odor of fresh water, of the future, of the journey's end and the challenge's failure.

The children look out the window and see only sunlight.

Mr. Jefferson's lover reaches one of her long and slender hands out the open window to snap off a twig from one of the giant trees growing just outside. The sun strikes the creamy skin of her wrist like something spilled. She hands the little branch to Mason and Alice's youngest daughter and tells the group that this tree, a massive-trunked Osage orange planted by Mr. Jefferson himself, is grown from a single cutting brought back by Lewis and Clark from their 1803–5 expedition to explore the Louisiana Purchase. "You may have this," she tells the girl.

"You may take it home and plant it, wherever you live, and perhaps someday two hundred years from now your tree will be as revered and significant as this one is now, carried so far to be planted by a caring hand, so long ago."

Their daughter, shy with the sudden notoriety, thanks her. The guide has no way of knowing that Mason and Alice are from eastern Montana, that they live along the Missouri River, probably not far — a dozen miles? fifty? — from where this specimen was first gathered. What unseen hand, or ghost, guides her to choose them as the recipient of this small symbolism? To carry a tree across parts of three centuries, and an entire continent and that continent's wars, only to have the tree turn around and head right back to where it started from, as if those two-hundred-plus years of this one Osage orange's journey had all been a mistake in the first place?

Into the final room, the end of the tour. Their daughters take turns clutching the souvenir of the Osage orange. Into the Tea Room, where there are the busts of sixty-four American heroes and friends, including Jefferson's beloved wife, Martha Wayles Skelton Jefferson.

"After what Mr. Jefferson called 'ten years of unchequered happiness,'" their guide tells them, "Martha dies at the age of thirty-four from complications resulting from childbirth. Family accounts report that she was vivacious, intelligent, attractive, and musical. 'A single event wiped away all my plans and left me a blank which I had not the spirits to fill back up,' Mr. Jefferson wrote. But he did fill them back up. Slowly," the guide says, "slowly, but they filled back up."

What did Mason know, when he first came here, so long ago? He was sixteen. He was asleep. He would be awakened; he would fall back asleep. He tried to stay awake for as long as he could. He tried to hold on to love for as long as he could. In the end it proved to be vaporous, ungraspable: as elusive as any impassioned dream.

The tour is over. Their guide slips from them with nary a farewell nor conclusion. She wanders down into the forest to commune with the spirits. Her dress is damp against her. They cannot see the blue elk, nor can she; it scents her coming and moves away from her, farther into the woods. She can feel the heat of its presence, where it was, and in the woods, following this heat, she trails it, squinting and trying to remember, and still hoping, still hoping as a young woman or even a girl hopes.

4

He built on a hill, a mountaintop, where the view was sublime, but where, of course, there was no water. This from a man who had said, "No occupation is so delightful to me as the culture of the earth, and no culture so comparable to that of the garden."

The gardens and orchards were kept watered, certainly. Catchment basins were carved in the stony cranium of the mountaintop, and wells were hammered out, blow by blow, as if to the center of the earth, deep wells that ran dry each day after only a few buckets and which recharged too slowly, as the mountain seeps and springs filled gradually back in on themselves, as if some slow weeping were occurring underground. He was so rich and gifted above the ground, but so impoverished below.

Daffodils, monk's hood, sea kale, and pear trees, and a thousand other thirsty drinkers, in the gardens and orchards — those desperate willows! — as well as the thirsting demands of the human household, and the many slaves, and the stock. It was so much more than the mountain could give.

Those pear trees, whose blossoms fly through the air like handfuls of flashing fish scales? That beauty, and all the mansion's beauty, was dreamed by Mr. Jefferson but crafted by the hands and feet, the muscled labor, of the slaves.

Mason and Alice stare at all the beauty, sensing some disparity, some incongruousness — something like horror metamorphosed across the centuries into beauty — like blooming love vine growing from the rotting carcasses of an old fallen tree, or even the corpse of a fallen soldier — and yet still they cannot name or grasp the specifics of the wrong, so stark and soothing is the great beauty in which they stand.

They know that the past was wrong, but where, in the present, amidst such beauty, can anyone see that wrongness? They can sense the echo of it beneath the soil and in their blood and in their minds, but they cannot see it.

They leave the mansion, in the green light of spring — those petals blowing past them now like confetti thrown at the loveliest of weddings — and stop and peer down into the depths of one of the wells, next to the slave quarters.

There's a grate welded over the top of the well to prevent people from falling inside, and their girls kneel before the grate and drop pebbles down into its vast darkness.

They can barely see the glint of the still water so far, far below. (The well is not used anymore; water is instead piped uphill from the Shenandoah River.)

They count the long, long moments it takes for each pebble to plink into the sky's reflection far below. It's astounding how deep the searchers had had to dig to arrive at even that meager and distant trickle; and in the number of seconds it takes for each pebble to splash, and in the distance of time it then takes for the sound of that splash to travel back up to them, the listeners above can measure precisely the frustration, and sometimes perhaps even terror, Mr. Jefferson must have felt, night and day, that he had built his home, his life, his dream, on a substrate that was not adequate for either his needs nor his desires.

How many countless days, and then years, was water instead hauled, bucket after bucket, from the distant shining river at the base of the mountain — hauled bucket by bucket in an endless and ceaseless procession of brute labor — curl of deltoid, sheen of broad back, and laboring mule?

Such folly! A beautiful edifice, but he should never have built here.

The girls take turns clutching their little twig. As Mason remembered next to nothing from his first trip to Monticello, what, in turn, will they remember?

Perhaps the light through the old glass. Perhaps the giant Osage orange tree, or perhaps the dry clink the pebbles made as they tumbled all the way down the nearly dry well to the distant water so far below. Waiting, in their child's game, to hear the tiny *plink!*, as long ago the anxious dreamer himself, with far less pleasure, might have leaned over this very well and listened likewise, watching and waiting for the well to recharge, so slowly, with so much other beauty all around him.

Mason and Alice glance at each other nervously. Always, Mason tells himself, we should remember what is at stake. Our little slaves.

Something catches the corner of his eye: some distant movement, back in the woods. Something blue and wild and powerful.

He turns away.

Two Deer

It was January when the first deer went through the ice. I was out in the barn working, and Martha came running out of the cabin to tell me.

I grabbed a rope and went running down to the lake. The deer, a doe, had gone out onto the new ice, all the way to the middle, and had crashed through. It was twenty below and supposed to get colder. The deer had punched a car-sized hole in the center and was swimming in circles, flailing and trying to pull herself up onto the ice with her black shiny hooves. She would work her front legs up and prop herself on the ice that way, like a woman resting her elbows at a table, and then she would kick and thrash, trying to pull herself back up, but would crash through again and slide back into the water. Then she would resume swimming in circles, panicked.

I hurried out onto the ice. The ice cracked under my feet; I slowed down. I knew my wife was watching from the window and I could feel her thinking, *stupid, stupid,* as I went out across the ice. We had a new baby.

The doe's eyes widened. She swam harder, certain that I was coming to leap on her back and bite her neck. The ice was making splintering sounds, so I got down on all fours and crept closer. I was almost close enough to throw the rope.

One knee punched through the ice, and I sank into the water up to midthigh. I lay spread-eagled to keep from sinking any deeper. Cold water swirled around my chest. I could feel the cake of ice I was lying on breaking away from the rest; it began to bob and float, and then sink. I figured I was going down as well, and it was a sour feeling to realize Martha and baby were watching me. I hoped they weren't filming me; we had gotten a new video camera because of the baby, and Martha was always filming everything. It would be a stupid death, captured on tape.

I rolled onto my back — water rushing all around me — and wriggled backwards from the floating ice onto the firmer shelf ice behind me, sliding away from the hole in the ice, away from the thing I was trying to save.

The deer was, I'm sure, wondering only if it would go under or be leapt upon.

The second deer leapt in front of my headlights in March. Another doe, it just came sailing up over a snowbank. Her feet never touched the road. I slammed on the brakes and tried to swerve but hit her in mid-flight, as if she were a bird. The truck struck her left shoulder and knocked her into the snowbank.

I stopped the truck and got out and picked up her limp body, and loaded her into the back of the truck with my dogs. She was heavy, and I had to wonder if she was pregnant from back in the fall, from the wild rut that goes on in November, deer chasing each other all over the place, a carnival of deer breeding.

The day before I hit the doe had been the first mild day since winter, the first one where you could feel the sun again, and I'd noticed all the animals walking around slowly, blinking and standing out in meadows as if marveling that such a thing as sun and grass, and open ground, existed.

This deer had eluded starvation, coyotes, and lions, had survived the long hard winter, and now I had snuffed her out, here on the cusp of spring. All of that brave suffering had been for nothing.

My dogs were in the back of the truck with her. It was just into nightfall — seven o'clock. At first the dogs were excited by the deer, but once we started down the road they calmed some, and by the time we got to the cabin those sweet hounds had moved over next to the deer and were lying with their heads resting on her shoulder and flanks, as if keeping her warm. I saw with some surprise that the deer had her head up and was looking around.

I whistled the dogs out and shone a light on the deer. She had just a little bump on her head, and I left the tailgate open, hoping she would jump out and run back into the woods. It was a clear night with stars, and later I crept out and laid a heavy blanket over her. I kept checking on her through the night.

Gradually her head went lower and lower, though, and her breathing grew more ragged. She began to cough, and in the morning she was dead, stiff, her eyes shaded to a dull and opaque blue.

I pulled her out of the truck and took her behind the barn and cleaned her. I was slightly sickened to discover upon gutting her that her shoulder was shattered hopelessly and that her stomach lining had ruptured, so that all of her intestines and other organs (except for the heart) had slid down into the lower half of her body. It was a terrible mess. And she'd just been holding up her head like nothing was wrong. It was dumb to think she could've been all right. I could scarcely believe, looking at her, my childish hopes of the night before — that she might hop down out of the truck and go back off into the woods, and survive, even prosper. I cleaned her and hung her in the barn to age for five days.

The third deer ran through my yard the very next day. I was in the barn trying to work, huddled over a quickly cooling cup of coffee, and I heard the dogs barking the way they do when they see coyotes. They were snarling and barking — Ann howling like a wolf — and I jumped up and ran out into the snow, nearly colliding with this deer, which was bounding through the deep drifts.

A big coyote was right on its tail, and my dogs were chasing the coyote as it chased the deer. We all arrived at the same place at the same time.

The coyote stopped in his tracks when he saw me, but the deer kept going. The coyote whirled and ran in the opposite direction. The dogs chased him a short distance, then turned and trotted back.

I felt like I'd saved that deer, which helped dull the guilt I'd been feeling about the other deer, but it wasn't an altogether clean trade, because I knew that coyotes had to eat. I had saved the deer but had messed up the coyote.

Our lives move deeper and slower — as if they are taking on weight. It's good weight, most of it, but it alarms us, I think, at the way it feels like that added weight tries to sink us.

It's like sinking through snow up to your ankles, or deeper. It's like not being sure, one day, that the ice will hold you — when every day before, it has. It may be my imagination, but it seems like Martha doesn't want to talk about this — perhaps does not even believe that this accrual of weight is happening. As if she believes that any day now — tomorrow, for instance — things will begin to get lighter and freer again — if she would even admit to this weight-gathering occurring in the first place.

Martha says all things are cyclic, and they are, but this thing — us — is somehow different.

The things outside of us seem never to change, beyond the constancy of the four seasons — birth, life, death, rebirth — but I'm convinced that our lives are different, just a tad above or below these constant cycles. As if we are on some march through the woods toward some final, newer place.

But Martha won't listen to this kind of talk. She says it's all one cycle, that nothing's changing. And still: despite the endlessness of the days, there are fractures and gaps where whole chunks of time will fall away — as if calving away from the core. Things that were assumed to lock-solid, rock-sure, weaken and fall away, leaving only loss, emptiness, and confusion.

And we start anew.

The thing that gets the deer in these woods most of the time is the wolves. There's usually just one pack at a time in this little valley. They keep the deer pruned back real nice, real healthy. None of our deer has ticks or other parasites. Nature's still working the way it's supposed to up here.

There are a lot of coyotes, too, but if the wolves find the coyotes in their territory they kill them as well, viewing the coyotes as competitors. We've seen a group of four wolves chase a pack of a dozen coyotes across a meadow, routing them.

Coyotes hunt the same prey as wolves but use a different style. The coyotes aren't as efficient as the wolves — a lot of times they'll only try to injure a deer, then stay near it for days, waiting for it to succumb — whereas the wolves just pretty much go after what they want and either get it or don't. And if they get it, they get almost all of it. They'll eat nearly everything — 85 percent, 90 percent, sometimes 100 percent of the kill — bones, hooves, hide, everything. As if the thing never was.

Summer, and our slow days around the cabin: cutting some firewood to sell, or building rock walls for the neighbors; in the late summer, both of us canning fruit and making jam. The heat almost unbearable, boiling water on the wood stove, with which to sterilize the fruit jars. Huckleberries from the woods, and strawberries from the garden. Sweat pouring down us. Adding half a bag of sugar to the whole vat. Pouring it steaming into the jars, and sealing them, and then waiting for the lids to *pop!*, indicating they've swelled to a perfect tight seal. The sweat veeing down our chests and backs; the crackle of the fire in the wood stove, and the baby asleep in the bedroom. Martha and I slipping down to the pond, undressing, and going for a swim to clean off. Making love in the pond — too hot out in the sun — and then climbing up onto the bank to dry in the faintest of breezes — late August, September — and no sound in the world, other than the silence of the baby sleeping and the faintest leaf clatter of the aspens — the sound of a cloud — and the irregular, soothing *pop* of each fruit jar.

Winter at full arm's length: coming, but still a full arm's length away. Dry brown grasses drying in the sun; our lazy arms around each other, our milky skin. A ninety-day growing season.

The deer that I hit with the truck, and carried home — the one that I hung out in the barn: on the fifth day of aging it, I went out to butcher her. I'd been walking past to check her every day — to make sure the coyotes hadn't gotten her. And every day when I'd gone by, the deer had been untouched. The doe had been hanging there the same as I'd left her, with her back to me, neck outstretched by the rope, hanging from the rafters with all four legs drooping at her sides, drawn by gravity.

I'd assumed she was still all there, and I'd begun to look forward to the meat. I was going down to the desert to camp and was looking forward to baking the two big glistening red loins in the coals of a campfire, and I was going to marinate great long red strips of the backstrap.

I went into the barn with the butcher knife, but when I swung the doe around to begin skinning the hide, the carcass felt as light as a coat on a coat hanger, and as I spun her to face me I saw that there was only a skeleton beneath the hide, that a coyote had gotten into the barn and had eaten the meat off of her hindquarters, had eaten out all of the butt steaks, had eaten up into the carcass as far as it could reach — standing on its hind legs to do so — eating all the way up to the bottom half of the backstrap, so that only the shoulders and neck were left untouched. I was stunned, and ashamed. I thought I knew better. You can't keep a coyote away from meat. It'll get it — whatever it takes, it'll get it, just as the wolves do.

Martha studied whitetails in college, got her doctorate in ungulate nutrition, specialized in winter range requirements. We used to talk about deer all the time — about almost nothing but deer. The bucks we'd seen. When we thought the fawns would drop. When the rut would start: that one week of the year when the bucks run wild, dashing through the forest day and night looking for does to breed, intent on only one thing. Totally unaware of their mortality. Road-hunters cruising the snowy lanes in big trucks, knocking down the bucks as the bucks run right past them, ignoring the trucks, ignoring everything but the sweet scent of deer vulva and buck jism, which has always reminded me of the holidays.

Roadside gut piles and gleaming red carcasses left behind then, and coyotes slipping out of the woods to join in the feast, and ravens cawing all over the valley in what can only be called pagan glee, swooping in and out of the trees with gobbets of red flesh dangling from their beaks, and the snow coming down, sealing off the old world and making the new one, the clean white beautiful one . . .

Martha and I met in college. I was studying civil engineering at a small school in northern Utah. I'd gone there for the skiing. I was going to learn how to build roads into the forest. I was eighteen years old; what did I know better?

Martha was eighteen, too. She explained to me that what I was doing was bad, that road-building in the West destroyed the last pieces of wilderness, fragmented the last sanctuaries where the wild things — the bears and the wolverines, caribou and great gray owls — holed up and hid out from man's hungry, clumsy, stupid ways.

She told me that we had too many roads already, that the mountains and all wildness was disappearing beneath concrete, and that what I needed to be learning to do instead was to tear up old roads and plant trees in their place.

It took me about two weeks to change my major. And I have to say it probably wasn't her passionate defense of centuries-old forests falling to bulldozers, or soil sloughing into pristine brooks. It was her ass that converted me.

But it's not as if I followed her like a puppy; I steered clear of her wildlife science classes, her ecofeminism curricula. I changed to literature. When she went out on her wolf howlings (thirty fucking below, in January) I usually stayed in town, at the library. I would read a life while she lived one.

This isn't to say we weren't in love. We were, as much as any two young people are capable of, which is to say, a lot. Our differences — the way she was so outgoing, the way her energy poured out of her, like water over a spillway, and the way I held mine all in — these differences formed a lock on us, the way deer and wolves fit together in the woods: one's movements always affecting the other's.

What I did with that first deer — the one that fell through the ice in January — was run back to my cabin and dig my canoe out from under the snowdrifts.

Drenching wet, but with my clothes starting to freeze in that clanking wind, I dragged the canoe down to the lake and slid it onto the ice. I sledded it out to where the ice began to crack and splinter, and then I got in the canoe, and began to smash the ice with my paddle.

The deer's eyes rolled wild as I broke that ice, and I sledged my canoe, a foot at a time, closer.

Finally, I had the canoe off of the ice and out into the open water, the cold black water. I canoed right up to the swimming deer — the deer so cold, and tired — and slipped the noose over its head. I hauled it up out of the water and managed to haul it into the canoe with me. It scrambled, trying to leap free, but I gripped the rope tight and held on.

With my free arm I paddled us back in the ice-breaking lane I'd plowed on my way out — a lane just wide enough to slip a canoe through.

Once on shore, I pulled the deer out of the canoe and put it over my shoulders. I carried it up the mountain and then turned it loose deep in the woods, in a cedar jungle where I knew there were neither wolves nor coyotes — too thick and tangley for them. I watched the deer run off. The ice had frozen into a glass coat around the deer, and as the deer ran, the ice shattered and tinkled. It was like a kind of miracle.

I remember us driving through town one day, the whole family — Martha and me and the baby — on a shopping trip and to see a movie. It was in the winter, and too far to drive all the way back that night; we'd gotten a hotel room in town and would head back the next day, up over the snowy pass.

It was right around Christmas. The lights were twinkling, and streamers and banners were draped across Main Street. There were snow-flecked wreaths on the doors of all the businesses. We were coming back from the movie theater when we saw a hunter driving home with a deer strapped to the hood of his car. He was doing it mostly to show off: just cruising the main drag. The clank of tire chains on the snowy road. Smoke rising from everyone's chimney.

There was no need to be parading that thing around. The guy was just being an asshole.

Still, it was a big deer. It's possible it was some kind of record deer — some kind of trophy.

The guy pulled over in front of the Chevrolet dealership and got out and stretched: an excuse for people to stop and ask him about that big deer, to comment on his prowess, etc.

We walked over to look. Snow was falling. Everything was real nice and quiet. There was that nice hush, the sense of community, of seasons and change and closure, that always comes near the end of deer season, in the West, in the mountains: the way autumn gives itself up to winter.

But this deer wasn't ready for any of that. No spirit mumbo-jumbo, no ghostly wraith-of-the-forest relinquishing itself back to the spirit of the wild; nor was there to be any edification of the sense of the rural community and its place in the hunting-and-gathering cycle of things on the account of *this* deer, this snowy night, because this deer wasn't dead. It was just knocked out.

The hunter had knocked him down, aiming for a heart-and-lung shot to keep from spoiling the trophy head, but out in the woods (he was telling us all this) the deer had jumped up again and charged him. The hunter had fired a second shot from the hip, striking the deer in the skull, dropping it instantly. Miraculously, the second shot didn't even break the skull or shatter the antlers.

That had been at dusk. The hunter had started to clean the deer, but it had gotten dark, and the hunter had decided to do that in town. Wanted to get his picture taken with a whole deer, not some diminished bloodstained gutted thing.

The cold ride off the mountain had revived the deer, however. The concussion wore off as we were all standing around admiring it. The great buck lifted his head like some European stag, and started kicking and thrashing. It slipped out of the ropes that had it fastened to the hood. It slid off the hood and bounded down the street. It ran down the sidewalk and past the bank. The electronic sign on the bank building said 7:03, and eight degrees.

The hunter looked as if he'd just had his own guts pulled out. I thought he was going to howl. The baby started laughing and pointing in the direction the deer had gone.

The tracks were easy to follow in the new snow. The hunter grabbed his rifle and started after the deer. The hole in the deer's side had opened again and was leaving glittering drops of crystalline blood, crimson as berries, which were already starting to freeze. It was just a little blood that the deer was leaking, but the wound would open up and bleed more as he kept running.

I knew this. The hunter knew this. We all knew it. Sometimes we know the language of deer perhaps as well as we know each other.

We all followed the hunter at a trot — the crowd of us, like a posse: men, women, and children.

It was as if the deer belonged to the whole community. It was a sense of loss for all of us when that deer leapt up and ran away. Only the baby was laughing. Her cheeks were rosy-red from the cold. She was clapping her mittens as we trotted along behind the hunter.

"How old is she?" one woman asked Martha as she ran alongside us.

The deer ran as if it knew where it was going; as if it had been in town before. It ran in a straight line, north, as if heading for the train station. Close to the mill, and close to the river.

The deer was starting to bleed more. We tracked the deer down to the end of Main Street and past the train station, across the railroad tracks and into the brush. It was headed for water, as any wounded animal will do.

Someone had a flashlight and turned it on as we hurried through the brush. Cold alder branches popped us. A few in the posse turned back, then: they had supper to cook, or bowling practice. Only about half a dozen of us kept on, having a strong interest in the way things would turn out.

The deer was losing more blood. How much blood did it have?

We found where the deer had slipped and had tried to rest for a moment, but it must have gotten back up when it heard us coming. If it had been my deer I wouldn't have pushed it so hard, would have let it go off and lie down to rest and die in peace, and then I would have tracked it, but it wasn't my deer.

He was going to push it all the way to the river.

There was no way the deer would be able to swim the river. The current was too fast, and the water too deep.

The tracks went straight out across the gravel bar, disappearing then into the dark river.

"He's in heaven now," a woman said. We were all breathing jets of silver puff-clouds. The mill's whistle moaned for the day shift to get off.

"He was *real*," the hunter said, near tears. He turned to us. The black river behind him seemed to stretch forever, laughing, now that that warm deer was in its cold belly.

"Did you all see it?" the hunter asked. He lifted his rifle, brandished it. "I want you all to know I shot that deer," he cried. "I did it, I was the one. For a while, I had it lashed to the hood of my car," he said. *"Me."*

Most of us looked away, disgusted. Maybe he had wounded that big old deer, and he'd probably even killed it — and maybe it was a record of some kind — but he'd lost it, too, and it's a sin to waste meat.

"Shit," said the woman who'd told us the deer was in heaven, "that doesn't count for *fuck*. I used to be in love with my husband, too — my ex — but *used to* doesn't count for shit."

A hunter in Idaho, seventy miles downstream, saw the icy corpse go floating by and retrieved it — lassoed it and dragged it in. He built a fire and thawed it out, took the carcass in to be measured, and it was true, it was the third largest whitetail ever shot, but he wouldn't give the deer back, so nobody got the record. We saw the picture of it in the paper.

There were some among us who believed the deer had not drowned when it hit the water, but had somehow swum that whole seventy miles, and *then* had drowned. In the long run it doesn't really matter, the deer's dead, but I'm one of the ones who believes he almost made it: that he swam that frigid river with his head, and that huge rack, out of the water, plumes of ice-rime ghosting from his nose, swimming through the lonely cold night; swimming for his life, his head held high: and he almost made it; almost.

We live in one of those places I did not build a road into. A place of wildness and mystery. Our little girl looks out the window on a winter morning and watches a family of otters playing on the river ice. There are elk outside, looking in the kitchen window, like missionaries who've come to visit. In my dreams, I think of our bodies as being the color of flames, because for half the year, it's so cold that the only place we can make love is in front of the fire, so that our writhing bodies take on the color of the fire itself. The skin at the ends of our fingers splits and cracks from the dryness of the cold. Our eyelashes sheet with frost when we go outside to ski or snowshoe. Ravens float above us when we ski, as if lonely for company in the huge silences.

We're shifting. I tend to be the effusive one now, prone to gushes of euphoria followed by torrents of despair, while Martha seems to have reversed and become the sane one, the steady one, the wise one.

The country behind us, through which we have traveled, and through which I don't guess we'll be traveling again: I can see it now, lying slightly below us.

Like so many of us, Martha loves the big predators, which are generally much more intelligent than their prey: the wolves, bears, and lions. She says that hunting is "the primary act of evolution that has most shaped the organic body we call intelligence." That's how she's always talked, and I've gotten used to it. Her language, in its own way, carries just as much passion as that of a poet's. It's just that her passion's hidden behind those awful words (*evolution,* and *organic body of intelligence*). It's all held in. She'll lay something like that on me, and I'll say, "Oh, you mean the predators have evolved larger brains to hold all the different data, all the possibilities they need to factor in to hunt with — the wind, slope gradient, temperature, soil conditions, sun's angle, moon's phase, and all of the other invisible things that are the very beat, the very pulse of the earth's skin itself?" And then she'll think I'm making fun of her.

Or she used to think that. But now she's becoming less and less interested in her science and more tolerant of mystery.

She hasn't learned it — mystery — from me. I think she has learned it from the deer, and the woods.

And I — for the first time — want to know a few answers, a little science, a little precision. Like, *What is going on? Where is it all going to end?*

What are our lives going to be like, from here on out? I'd like a little direction for once, a little glow at the end of the tunnel.

So many things can end a deer's existence. Not just predation, but also starvation, malnutrition, liver flukes, worms. Smaller things, a series of events that lead to a gradual deterioration in the deer's well-being — a series of mistakes, or harshnesses of nature, are generally what leads to the end of the line. But it's all part of a flow. I see that, living up here in the mountains. I see it in the ways of deer, and in the ways of the seasons, and I see it in us, too. It's neither good nor bad: it just *is*.

Martha's doctorate work included studies about the nutrition a deer needs when the going gets really rough. She would measure cell wall content of forbs as a percentage of dry matter; would measure lignocellulose content, and the nitrogen in dead vegetation in winter, and she would formulate digestibility factors for the deer. The rains of fall and snows of winter degrade the cell walls and leach nitrogen from the plant tissues. I like to think of it as the land taking back those elements that it had loaned to the deer for the summer, for the joy of that quick life. Martha's old technical papers tend to express it a bit more dryly:

"Calcium has a large role in blood clotting as well as maintaining neuromuscular excitabilities and in the acid-base equilibrium of the body. Dietary calcium at a level of 0.40% of dietary dry matter in the presence of 0.25–0.28% phosphorus is adequate for postweaning fawns. Chlorine occurs in body fluids, where it helps regulate osmotic pressure and maintain tissue pH levels . . ."

But in the long run, I want to know about the mystery of it, not the fucking pH of it. Now I want to know about the roadless areas.

She used to do autopsies on winter-killed deer that people would bring in to the university. For some deer the causes of death were obvious: the brittle bones of selenium deficiency, or the puncture marks in the neck from coyotes' teeth. But for others, so many others, there appeared to be no reason for dying. They had just stopped living. It was as if there were something out there that could not be measured: a thing they needed but had run out of.

I remember the year when Martha said she didn't love me

anymore. The baby was seven. The baby is a genius, we think. We knew it even then. She learned to read by the time she was three, and she could also tell the difference between a buck track and a doe track. She's an utter joy to be around. She, as much as the beautiful landscape around us, reminds us to love one another. But that year when Martha flat-out told me she didn't love me anymore — that was a tough one.

You can't manufacture love: you can't build it back up, like a fire. You start out with a certain amount, and then hope it is strong enough and lasting enough to sustain itself against the hard winters, and the assault of time. And it changes; it fluctuates — it gets either stronger or weaker. And sometimes all of the center can just go out. That core, that base, can just get cold, and stay cold, for too long. It's one of the dangers.

It got right down to the very end. I was going to leave. It was as if my guts were open: as if ravens and eagles were already feeding on my heart. Still, I was going to let her — them — go. Off to that new direction in life that would not include me anymore.

But we muscled through it; somehow we got back into love, or were perhaps carried back into it, unconscious, on a sled, as if pulled through the night by some higher being. The spring came, and we were still alive, and when the woods and meadows turned green again, we started to love each other again.

A harsh winter like that one never came back. Or has not, yet.

Martha and I went on a field trip once, up the North Fork of the Whiteflesh River in northern Montana: right where the country crosses over into Canada. It was for a wolf study project that

Martha's class was doing. We were supposed to follow a thirteen-mile transect due north and count how many moose, how many deer, how many elk. We were supposed to howl every 400 meters and count the wolves that responded.

It was on Thanksgiving Day. It had snowed hard the day before, two feet, and then dropped to twenty below.

We had to cross the river naked: holding our clothes over our head to keep them dry, and then build a warming fire on the other side of the river. It was madness and euphoria.

It was so beautiful. The salmon sky, snow clouds between us and the sun, cast a pearly reddish-goldish light, as if we were in some new stage of heaven. All day long there was a light on our faces almost like firelight. The snow was frozen hard in places, so that we could walk across it like concrete for two or three steps, but then we'd hit a soft or weak spot that our feet would punch through, and we'd collapse up to our waists. It was exhausting work. But we were so in love: *so in love.*

We came across a small pond back in the woods that was completely frozen. Wolf tracks led us to the pond and to the dead deer that was out on the pond: nothing left to it but a few bones. Even the ravens had finished with this carcass.

"That's how they do it," Martha explained. "The wolves try to get the deer out onto the ice where the deer will slip and go down, or will even punch a leg through and get stuck.

"Then the wolves move in." She made a whistling sound, drew her finger across her throat. "And then it's over."

We examined the bare bones and the tracks of the wolves; the brushed-out areas of snow where the ravens' wingtips had swept across the snow. The pittery-pat markings of the coyotes that had come in to lick and crunch the bones after the wolves were through.

We continued north, then, into the beautiful day. There was some undefinable essence out there that day, which seemed to shout, simply, in the name of every mountain and every river, every deer and every wolf, that Martha and I belonged together, under that odd lingering salmon sky. I have never forgotten that day, that feeling, and I still hold on to it.

Because you love wolves or other predators, you have to study their food source, which is deer. It's like learning to play the piano before you learn to play any other kind of music. You must understand deer long before you can understand wolves or anything else. I understand this, though still it strikes me as odd, mysterious.

It seems like trying to say "I love you" without using the word "love." It's like trying to say, "It doesn't matter how much you change, or I change, we will always be in this country together, and whatever changes come, whatever mysteries, will be as wonderful and scary as they have always been."

It's like trying to say, "Let's not let each other become small or weak or diminished." It's like saying, "There will always be some amount of ice beneath us."

It's like saying, "We must go on, I love you, there is no choice."